D0937483

Wild
REBEL

Hot Alphas. Smart Women. Sexy Stories.

Wild
REBEL

NEW YORK TIMES BESTSELLING AUTHOR

LAURELIN PAIGE

paige press

Copyright © 2021 by Laurelin Paige

All rights reserved.

No part of this book may be reproduced in any form or by any electronic or mechanical means, including information storage and retrieval systems, without written permission from the author, except for the use of brief quotations in a book review.

Paige Press, LLC
Leander, Texas

ISBN: 978-1-953520-37-1

Editing: Erica Russikoff at Erica Edits

Proofing: Michele Ficht, Kimberly Ruiz

Cover: Laurelin Paige

ALSO BY LAURELIN PAIGE

Visit my website for a more detailed reading order.

The Dirty Universe

Dirty Filthy Rich Boys - READ FREE

Dirty Duet (Donovan Kincaid)

Dirty Filthy Rich Men | Dirty Filthy Rich Love

Dirty Games Duet (Weston King)

Dirty Sexy Player| Dirty Sexy Games

Dirty Sweet Duet (Dylan Locke)

Sweet Liar | Sweet Fate

(Nate Sinclair) Dirty Filthy Fix (a spinoff novella)

Dirty Wild Trilogy (Cade Warren)

Wild Rebel | Wild War | Wild Heart

Man in Charge Duet

Man in Charge

Man in Love

Man for Me (a spinoff novella)

Written with Kayti McGee under the name Laurelin McGee

Miss Match | Love Struck | MisTaken | Holiday for Hire

Written with Sierra Simone

Porn Star | Hot Cop

Be sure to **sign up for my newsletter** where you'll receive **a FREE book every month** from bestselling authors, only available to my subscribers, as well as up-to-date information on my latest releases.

Pro Tip: Add laurelin@laurelinpaige.com to your contacts before signing up to be sure the list comes right to your inbox.

DID YOU KNOW...

This book is available in both paperback and audiobook editions at all major online retailers! Links are on my website.

If you'd like to order a signed paperback, my online store is open several times a year here.

Paige Press isn't just Laurelin Paige anymore...

Laurelin Paige has expanded her publishing company to bring readers even more hot romances.

Sign up for our newsletter to get the latest news about our releases and receive a free book from one of our amazing authors:

Stella Gray, CD Reiss, Jenna Scott, Raven Jayne
JD Hawkins, Poppy Dunne

ONE

I paced the length of Donovan's office, then checked my watch for the third time in as many minutes. She wasn't late yet, but there was a boulder of doubt in my stomach that had me sure she wouldn't come at all. It was a natural assumption after last time. How long had I waited that night? At what point had I known for sure that she was going to ghost?

I'd been more optimistic then. I'd waited hours. Now I relied on experience. If she were planning to show at all, the Jolie I'd known would have been early.

But I hadn't known her for a long, long time.

And the name was Julianna, not Jolie. No one called her Jolie but me, and I refused to call her that now. She didn't deserve it. In the week since I'd gotten her email, I'd practiced it over and over. *Julianna, Julianna, Julianna.* She wasn't Jolie anymore. Jolie disappeared the night I waited for her in a rundown pickup in the parking lot of a CTown Supermarket. Jolie was gone.

Again, I checked my watch. Not even thirty seconds had passed. Time was moving at a snail's pace. I cracked my neck from side to side before loosening my tie. I'd already taken off the jacket, and I was still sweating. It was a Saturday in December, for fuck's sake, and I was the only one in the Reach office. Did the guys keep the heater on over the weekends? No wonder the New York overhead was so high.

I crossed to the thermostat and was surprised to find it was actually set at an arctic temperature that only an asshole penny-pincher would have thought was acceptable, which made sense because Donovan and I were alike in that area. When we'd worked the office together in Tokyo, we'd had the trimmest budget of all the Reach locations. It had risen a bit when he'd moved to the States since I no longer had the time to keep a close eye on it. I hadn't really examined the New York numbers in a while, but I had a feeling they'd probably improved with his presence.

Regardless of company spending and the perspiration beading on my forehead, the current setting was not all that friendly. I'd be a bad host to leave it there. I considered doing just that before begrudgingly switching the heater on full blast. Hopefully, it would do something before Jolie showed up.

Not Jolie.

Julianna.

Fuck, this was a giant mistake. This whole thing. I shouldn't have opened the email. I shouldn't have responded. I shouldn't have told her I was going to be in New York for a wedding that I'd had no prior plans to attend. I most definitely shouldn't have dropped everything, boarded a plane, and flown halfway across the world to impatiently pace Donovan's office, waiting for her to show. Especially knowing she had a record for *not* showing.

If I'd been intent on justice, I would have ghosted *her* this time.

But it wasn't justice I needed most from Julianna Stark. It was closure. And that's why I was there—for me, not for her. And so help me God, if she'd stood me up again...

I forced myself to sit on the edge of the desk. It wasn't exactly a relaxed position, but it was better than wearing a hole in the carpet. Still antsy, I pulled out my phone and reread her email, even though I could recite it by heart without looking.

CADE,

I know I have no right to reach out to you like this, but there's no one else I can turn to...

MY GAZE SKIPPED down to her signature. She'd used the name I refused to call her. The one meant to tug at my emotions. Fuck her for that. Fuck her for all of it.

My agitation renewed, I stuffed my phone back in my pocket and took a deep breath. I refused to be riled up when she got here. With my palms settled on my thighs, I traced the tattoos on the back of my hands with my eyes. It was a trick I'd taught myself a decade or so ago, back when the pressure of some of my bigger jobs got the best of me, and I needed something to help me focus. I hadn't had to use it since going into business with Donovan and the guys. Advertising was definitely a high-stress career, but it was legit, and that made it a walk in the park compared to what I'd done before.

The trick still worked. By the fifth sweep of my eyes along the inked skin, I was breathing more regularly, and even though the heat had kicked in, I was feeling cool enough to reach for my jacket.

Just as I fastened the button of the navy blue Armani, I heard the ding of the elevator arriving. Then the sound of two sets of footsteps clicking on marble flooring echoed through the hallway.

She was here.

Fuck. She was here, and I was going to keep it together, whatever it took.

I ran my hand over my beard, straightened my tie, then with a final curse under my breath, I clicked the button that turned the glass wall from opaque to transparent and moved to stand in front of it.

There wasn't a direct path to the elevators from Donovan's office, so I had to wait until the pair turned down the corridor, and then it was Fran that I saw first, the security guard that I'd tipped a hundred in exchange for personally walking my guest to the back office. Was it necessary? Probably not. I told myself I was being hospitable. Truth was, I didn't want to be alone when we first saw each other.

And when Jolie—I'd given up on calling her Julianna in my head—followed Fran around the corner, I knew I'd made the right choice because, even with her head bent and her eyes fixed on the floor, Jolie was a lodestone, and I was fighting really hard not to be iron. If it had been just the two of us, I wasn't sure I would have been able to resist her pull.

I wasn't sure I'd be able to resist her pull even with Fran between us.

Thank God for the glass wall.

Showing up now doesn't make up for not showing up back then.

In case that wasn't enough of a reminder, I forced myself to remember what had happened when I'd gone after her. My ribs hurt with the vividness of that memory. My shoulder throbbed where the bone had once been broken. My chest ached with the pain of a fractured heart.

And just like that, her pull on me diminished.

"I think she has it from here, Fran," I called out. The glass was between us, but the office door was open, so I could be heard. "Thank you."

At the sound of my voice, both women came to a halt. Fran had already been looking at me, but my gaze settled past her, watching as Jolie's head lifted, her eyes swiftly meeting mine, and much as I told myself not to look for anything from the past in her face, I immediately saw the girl she'd been back then. Her cheekbones were sharper, sure. Her curves were more filled out, her naturally dark hair had been dyed blonde and cut to her shoulders, and I hadn't remembered her eyes being so light, and yet, I would have recognized her anywhere.

So much for convincing myself she was someone new.

"Sure, sure," Fran said with a tone that said she was positive she hadn't earned the generous tip I'd given. She lingered a couple of seconds, as though trying to decide if she should give the money back or make peace with the unbalance. "Tell you what—you let me know when you're on your way out, and I'll come back up for a thorough sweep and set the alarm for you."

"Will do." I could turn the alarm on and off with the push of a button on my phone, but if it made her feel good enough to leave, then fine. I'd wanted her there as a buffer, but the foolishness of that notion was clearly evident. Now as then, when Jolie was in the room, the only person I saw was her.

Her gaze seemed just as intent to stay locked on mine.

Seconds passed like hours. Vaguely, I was aware of Fran turning around, of the clop, clop, clop of her footsteps as she made her way back to the elevator. The ding of its arrival had sounded and gone silent before either Jolie or I said a word.

"Hi." She was the one who spoke first because I was a fucking chickenshit, though even through the glass, I could hear a rasp in her voice that said this likely wasn't easy for her either.

I cleared my throat as if I could clear the scratch in hers for her. "I'm sure you'll be more comfortable sitting down." I gestured for her to join me. It was smugly satisfying that she had to be the one to walk to me.

Her plump lips curved down, and she nodded, as though realizing the tone of this meeting had been set and with that nod she'd accepted it. "Yes. Sitting down for this is probably best."

The disappointment in her tone was jarring—apparently I hated it as much now as I had then—and for the briefest of moments, I wished I'd said something else, something more inviting, something sentimental.

But then I told myself to fuck that regret. This wasn't a nostalgic reunion. This was an ending, and the sooner we got to her asking for her favor, the sooner that conclusion would come.

I knew that, yet as she walked toward me with the same brisk energy she'd had when we were younger, I found myself wishing she would slow down so I could stretch this moment to its limits. It had to last forever. It had to make up for so much lost time.

Fuck, I was in trouble.

Disgusted with myself, I moved away from the glass and had made it to the bar by the time she came in. "Have a seat," I said, busying myself with empty glasses. "Can I get you something to drink?"

"Water would be fine."

I opened the mini fridge, happy to have an excuse to keep my back to her. "Sparkling or still?"

"Either."

I grabbed a bottle of sparkling for her and abandoned my impulse to pour a whiskey for myself. I needed to keep a clear head.

But then I had to get close enough to her to hand her the water, and suddenly I regretted not having the alcohol.

She'd taken her coat off and draped it on the back of the chair with her purse, but she was still standing, despite my invitation to sit, which somehow made it worse when I crossed to her. I would have preferred looming above her. I would have preferred to not have to look her in the eye. And though I purposely made sure we didn't have physical contact, I could feel the spark between us all the same, as though she was lightning and the bottle between our fingers was a rod, and every part of my body lit up like the Christmas tree in the building lobby.

I let go immediately and took a step back.

"Thanks." She didn't open the bottle. I stared where her fingers wrapped around the cylinder shape, noting the lack of a ring where one should be if she were married. That was satisfying, at least.

Except a bare finger didn't necessarily mean anything, and I didn't care about her marital status, and I definitely didn't want her thinking I did, so I pushed my eyes up to hers where I found her attention was completely on me. She took in every change in my appearance—the beard, the tats, the muscular build I'd worked for in my twenties, the hard expression that was permanently etched on my face. "You look good," she said finally.

I didn't look good. I was jet-lagged and haggard, but when she said it, I believed her because that was just what I'd always done, and old habits die hard. "You look the same."

She made a noise that could almost be called a laugh. "I don't, but thank you."

I shrugged, not sure how else to respond. She did look the same, in all the ways that mattered, and that was a real fucking problem for me. It kept me looking at her when I should have been looking anywhere else. It kept me standing within arm's reach when I should have been stepping away.

"I'm underdressed," she said, looking down at her jeans and sweater. It was definitely more casual than anything she'd ever worn as a teenager, but we'd spent most of those days in a school uniform, and her father dictated what she wore the rest of the time, so it was impossible to know what her true style would have been.

It fit her, I realized. Fit who I'd imagined her to have grown up to be, someone who didn't try to impress anyone. Someone who dressed for practicality and comfort. Someone who didn't care about anyone else's opinion.

Except maybe she cared about mine because she seemed to be seeking reassurance. While I didn't care about making her feel better, the comment begged a response. "You're dressed appropriately for the weather."

"I didn't expect to see you all decked out in a suit."

"I have a wedding after this," I reminded her. A wedding I wasn't going to make it to since it started in twenty minutes. But I hadn't really ever planned on going anyway.

"Oh, yeah. That's right." Instead of taking that as a cue to hurry this along and sit down, she scanned the room and strolled toward one of the bookcases. Immediately, she found the one picture on Donovan's shelf that included me. She smiled as she leaned in to study it, and fuck if that smile didn't do something profound to my insides. Like her lips were razor blades cutting through the darkest parts of me, letting in sunshine that had no business brightening the gloom.

I willed myself to shut it out.

And still I found myself standing behind her, looking at the image over her shoulder, trying to imagine what it was she saw that she thought deserved that grin. It was of the five of us guys —Donovan, Weston, Nate, and Dylan—all of us dressed in our best suits and puffing cigars.

"I never pictured you as a cigar smoker," she said.

Probably because I'd been a cigarette smoker when she'd known me. I'd quit more than a decade ago, but strangely I found myself jonesing for a cigarette now. Funny how people from the past brought you back to the person you were when you knew them.

I wondered if she'd quit as well or if she had a pack buried in that oversized purse of hers. It was tempting to ask just to have her dig it out and hand it over, just to feel my lips on something that she'd touched.

"We were celebrating," I said, trying to rein in my wandering mind.

"Celebrating what?"

"The opening of this office."

"Was this the first location you opened? You said you were in Tokyo."

I found the words spilling out before I could stop them. "We planned to have three locations from the beginning. New York opened first, then Tokyo three months later, and London a few months after that."

"A global phenomenon." She sounded proud, and I liked that.

I hated it at the same time. She had no right to be proud of me. She had no right to care how I'd turned out. She had no right to smell the way she did—familiar and new all at once, a scent that made my head cloud and my pulse race and my chest feel like it was breaking in two.

She turned her head toward me, and we were so close I could make out the spattering of freckles on her cheeks, the ones she'd always hated. The ones that formed a constellation in my sleep. "I always knew you'd end up someone important," she whispered.

I *had* been someone important. I'd been hers.

And that hadn't been enough for her.

Abruptly, I moved back. "How about you tell me what it is you need from me, *Julianna*?" I said her name pointedly, proud that I hadn't tripped over it when it crossed my lips.

She turned to face me, her tongue sweeping across her lower lip. "Actually, it's Jolie now. I didn't change it legally, but I may as well have. It's what I go by."

As difficult as it was to think of her by any other name, this new bit of info pissed me off. Unreasonably so. I'd been the only one to call her that once upon a time, and while I didn't expect to still get to indulge in that honor, I sure as hell wasn't happy about discovering that the honor now belonged to everyone.

I definitely wasn't calling her that now. "Whatever you want to go by, I have that wedding to get to, so if we could hurry this along..."

"Right. Sorry." She still had that ability to close off in an instant. Like someone pulling down the blinds. One minute you could see deep inside her, the next she was shut up tight.

For the best, I reminded myself.

But damn if I didn't need a cigarette.

She walked past me and sat primly on the edge of the chair, the way her father had always professed that proper young ladies should sit, her hands laid casually in her lap. I followed after her, circling behind the desk, but instead of sitting, I stood, my arms folded over my chest, a posture her father would most certainly have found disrespectful.

It was a belligerent stance on my part, one that Langdon Stark probably deserved more than she did, but in a lot of ways, Jolie and her father were inseparable in my mind. The complicated feelings I had for one of them more often than not extended toward the other.

Except that I'd never loved Headmaster Stark. That emotion had belonged to Jolie alone. Still did, I supposed, since there hadn't been anyone I'd said the word to since her.

Which was why I needed closure.

I nodded toward her, a silent prompt to get on with it.

"You probably want to be sitting for this," she suggested.

"I'm fine like I am."

"All right." She let out a sigh. "I, um. I need to ask you for your help."

She hesitated, so I prodded her on. "Something only I can help with, you said. I have to be honest—I'm curious. It's hard for me to believe I'm the only one you can turn to when I haven't seen or heard from you in close to two decades. Surely there are other men you've strung along since me. What could this favor possibly be?"

The barb did the trick. She stopped hedging and spit it out. "I need you to help me kill my father."

TWO

She was right—I should have been sitting down.

I sat now with a chuckle as I ran my hand over my beard. I was hearing things. "I'm going to need you to say that again. For a second there, I thought you said you wanted me to help you kill your father."

Her expression stayed even. "That's what I said."

I held her gaze, impossibly trying to read somebody that I used to know. She looked sincere.

But, hell, I'd thought she meant the things she said to me back then, too.

I pressed back in the chair as much as it would give. Donovan apparently preferred sitting straight and tall. I was more of a lean kind of a guy, but when *the* woman from my past was sitting in front of me asking the outrageous, the lack of mobility was a nuisance that barely registered. "What is this? Some kind of practical joke?"

"It's not a joke."

"You want to kill your father."

She shifted uncomfortably in her chair. "You don't have to keep saying it."

That almost had me laughing again. "You can't even hear it, and you think that's what you want. Nice try." Condescending, yes. I could be an ass, really without even trying.

Teenage Jolie wouldn't have stood for being patronized. Adult Jolie was a whole different organism. "It's not a decision I came to lightly."

"Well, that's heartening. A good murder plot really should involve at least one night of restless sleep."

She gave a sarcastic smile, then immediately dropped it. "Go ahead, get all the wisecracks out. I'll wait."

"It's not a wisecrack. This is not something to joke about."

"But you aren't taking me seriously."

I studied her for several seconds, sure I was still missing the punchline, but she remained somber, not a trace of humor anywhere in her countenance.

She was dead serious, no pun intended.

And I was thrown harder than I'd been thrown in years. "Fuck, Julianna. What do you expect me to say?" I was pretty sure that I couldn't even Google an appropriate response.

"It's Jolie," she corrected. "And you're right. It's brazen of me to be here at all, let alone to ask for you to help me with something so diabolical. But I hoped—I *hope*—that you will realize I wouldn't be here if I thought I had any other options."

"I'm a last resort, then." She'd basically laid that out in her email. And still, it stung. Stupidly. Like what answer would I have preferred? That she'd reached out because she needed me, and no one else could meet that need?

Obviously, I should have done a better job at managing my expectations.

She must have heard the bitterness in my tone. "I didn't mean..."

"No, I got it." Last thing I needed was a pitying platitude. Too fucking little, too fucking late. "I would never assume it was anything else."

Her mouth tightened, and as curious as I was to find out what comment she was biting back, I was more interested in controlling the conversation. Her silence gave me the reins, and with them, I took a hard turn. "Why?"

"Why...which part?" She crossed one jean-covered leg over the other, and I wondered if she knew how sultry she looked with the simple action or if she was completely unaware.

More likely it was the former. She'd known how to weaponize her femininity when she was just a kid. All these years later, I imagined she'd probably honed the skill.

I needed to remember that. That she'd never been innocent.

"How about we start with why you think you want your father dead?" I pointedly used the D word. I wasn't fucking changing my language to make her feel better. If she really was considering murder—which she couldn't be. Not really. The girl I knew wouldn't have been capable, and people didn't change that much—but if she was bold enough to be here talking about it out loud with a man who was, for all intents and purposes, a stranger, then she needed to be able to deal with the fucking terms.

Maybe she realized that, because though she cringed, she didn't remark on my choice of words. "You really have to ask?"

"Yeah. I really do."

"You, of all people, know what a monster he is."

"I know what a monster he *was*. Seventeen years ago."

"And you think he's changed?"

No, I didn't think he'd changed. Just like I didn't think she'd changed. But the fact of the matter was..."It's not my problem anymore."

She tsked. "That's not you. You're not that dismissive."

I wasn't sure what pissed me off more—her presumption that she knew shit about anything or her attempt to use it over me. "Don't pretend you fucking know anything about me. Do it again, and this conversation is finished." I managed to keep my voice low and steady, but there was no question that I'd drawn a line.

I half expected her to fall over herself with apologies or to take a step back. At least, try another tactic.

But she was Jolie fucking Stark, and backing down had never been her style. "It was an observation based on your actions. You tried to press charges against him a couple of years after..." She cleared her throat. "After you left."

It surprised me that she knew, but I refused to let on. "If you know that then you know that there was no case to be had. Might have been a different story if there had been someone to corroborate."

"They wouldn't have believed me any more than they believed you."

"I'm not sure how you could know that for sure without—"

She went on as if I hadn't spoken. "Which is why he has to be dealt with in other ways."

I could have argued the point further, but she was right. Not about murder, but about the limits of the law. The main reason my case was thrown out was because the accusations looked like an attempt at retribution against a man who hadn't wanted me anywhere near his daughter. Any charges Jolie brought up would have faced the same scrutiny.

And besides, she'd tried to report him once. Before I'd appeared on the scene. From what she'd told me, it was a mistake she had vowed not to make twice.

Once upon a time, that might have been reason enough for me to consider offing her old man. But all we'd had to do was make it to graduation to be free of him. We'd done that. We'd survived.

Then when she'd had the chance to walk away, she'd chosen to stay.

"So, next why—why now? You're an adult. You aren't living under his roof anymore. Not subject to his discipline. Surely you aren't just now concerned about what he might be doing to other students—"

"He didn't," she interrupted. "What he did to me—he wasn't like that with his students."

"Oh, right. It was just me." Lucky old me.

It wasn't completely true that it was just me and her who suffered. He might not have left physical marks on anyone else, but Headmaster Stark knew how to fuck with people in other ways. He was a true sadist—not particular about what methods he used to bring about agony, and I had no doubt that there were dozens, if not hundreds, of students who had suffered under his tutelage since our class.

Unfortunately, the mind fucking was even harder to prosecute than the physical abuse.

"I'll repeat the question—why now?"

For the first time since she'd dropped her bombshell, she looked away. "It doesn't matter."

"It sure as hell does. You want me to have this conversation with you, you at least have to have a motive."

Her head turned back toward me. "Isn't it better if I don't? No reason to suspect me."

"Yeah, that's not how it works. There obviously is a motive or you wouldn't be here, and I don't want to hear about it first from a cop who comes knocking at my door asking questions, so you might as well tell me now what they'd try to say." Not that I was seriously entertaining any of this.

"I guess they'd say I'd finally traced the source of all the shit in my life. Everything that has ever mattered to me, everything good that I've ever lost, it's been because of him."

God, she was good. With all the innuendo and subtext, wanting me to think she was talking about us. That she was talking about losing me. That right there was class A emotional manipulation.

Like father, like daughter, right?

"Have you lost something *recently*? Because if not, I'm going to ask once again—why now?"

She blinked once before answering. "It's complicated."

The fuck with *complicated*. It was a word I'd heard all my life—from my mother, from Jolie, from the lawyer who had tried to represent my case. I was tired of complicated being an excuse to end a conversation. I'd been tired of it so long that I had purposely set my life up to be simple. No ties. No obligations. Even my contract with the guys had a clear escape clause. Whatever I did, whomever I did it with, there was always a clear path out.

I didn't do *complicated* anymore, and if I was in my right mind, that would have been the moment to show her the door.

If I was in my right mind, I wouldn't have even answered

her email. Out of the blue, after all these years? It might as well have said "complicated" in the subject line.

Against better judgment, I was here.

Which led me to the most important why. "Why me?" I sat forward, suddenly afraid of the answer, and asked something better. "In fact, why anyone at all? You want the man gone, why not just do it yourself?"

"I can't figure out how. A registered gun is too easy to trace back to me, and I don't know the first thing about how to get one on the black market. I considered poisoning, but I don't have access to poison him, not on my own. Beyond that, I'm not creative enough to come up with a plan."

In other words, she wasn't a killer. Which I already knew.

"And when you realized you needed help, you thought, 'Who do I know who is capable of murder?' And then you thought, 'Oh, I bet Cade Warren would be up for that. He always did have that rebellious streak.' Should I be flattered?"

Really, I was surprised. Because I might have been trouble, but I hadn't been a guy who could kill back then. I'd come pretty close a couple of times, when the low-life job I'd had before Donovan "rescued" me had found me in some pretty shady circumstances, but that had been after Jolie. There wasn't any way she knew about that.

"I didn't reach out to you because I thought you'd be..." She let out a frustrated sigh. "That's not why."

"Then why? Why me, Julianna?"

She flinched at the name. "I thought two heads were better than one, and like I said before, you had reason enough to hate him."

"Reason to hate him? Yes. Reason to *kill* him?" I left that question unanswered because it shouldn't need voicing. Sure,

I'd imagined it enough times over my life. I'd imagined it in detail. I could write a book about all the ways I'd killed Langdon Stark in my head, but that didn't mean I'd ever actually do it.

"And if I did want the man dead," I went on, realizing there was another more pertinent part of this question, "why would I have waited nearly twenty years to do it? You couldn't have thought I was just sitting around waiting for someone to give me permission. If I'd wanted that motherfucker dead, he'd be dead. I wouldn't need you to tell me to do it."

"I know," she said solemnly. "I know I'm asking you to do this for no other reason than because I need someone to help me. I know I have no right. I know, Cade. I know."

"You know, and yet you're still asking."

"I am."

There was one more why—why did she think for one minute that I'd agree? But I didn't have to ask. The answer was right there, evident in her hopeful eyes and her pleading tone and her unsaid words. She thought I'd agree because she assumed that now, as then, I would do anything for her.

"You know what, Julianna? Nope."

"Nope?"

"Nope." After breaking her promise? After standing me up? After pushing me away, ignoring my attempts to reach out? After disappearing? After seventeen years? "Nope. And fuck you for even asking."

She drew back slightly. "I deserve that."

Yeah, she did. She deserved a whole hell of a lot more, as far as I was concerned.

"While we're at it"—I stood up, wanting the full advantage of my height—"fuck you for disappearing like you did. And fuck you for showing up out of the blue thinking that I owed you something—"

"I don't think that," she interjected.

"Then fuck you for thinking there was any chance in hell that I would do your dirty work for you—"

"Not *for* me. I'd do it with you."

"And fuck you for trying to sell that lie. To me. Of all people. You can't even squash a beetle under your shoe, and you expect me to think you could have any part of ending someone's life? It's bullshit. All of this is bullshit. I'm not going to be your fall guy—" She opened her mouth, and I put up a finger to silence her. "And I'm sure as fuck not going to be your knight in shining armor. I tried to play that part once, and I got burned. You don't know anything about the man that made me, so I'll lay it out—I'm not anyone's hero. But if I were going to start being one today, it sure as shit wouldn't be for Julianna Stark."

I hadn't planned to tell her off. As many times as I'd played it out in my daydreams, I hadn't wanted her to see me that affected. It was the weaker hand. Anger/hurt/resentment—showing any of those emotions proved she still had a hold on me, and while I knew she did, the last thing I'd wanted was for her to know that.

Despite that, it felt damn satisfying. Might have felt better if she'd broken down into tears, or, the jackpot, if she'd gotten down on her knees and begged, but her despondent silence was a hell of a gratifying end to our relationship. I was taking it as a win. A big fat fucking score.

Without saying anything, she reached out to Donovan's desk and grabbed a piece of paper off his notepad and a stray pen. "It's Jolie," she said as she jotted something down.

"Not ever calling you that."

She ignored the barb. "Here's my cell phone number." She set the paper and pen on the desk and stood before gathering her coat and her purse. "I'll be in town for a few days, if you change your mind."

"Not going to change—" But I was talking to her back now, so I didn't bother finishing the statement since she was obviously done listening.

Which made all that smug satisfaction fizzle away like a punctured tire. This was supposed to be *my* closure, and yet goddamned Julianna Stark had managed to once again have the last word.

THREE

P *ast*

I HISSED as I pulled my T-shirt over my head, then craned my neck, trying to see the marks on my back. They burned like a motherfucker, like my entire torso had been lit on fire, and though I couldn't see anything, I was sure I was probably bleeding.

Though my shirt was relatively clean. It was black, which made it hard to tell for sure, and the whole thing felt damp, but I'd been sweating. If I'd been wearing my uniform dress shirt like I was supposed to, I would be able to see better.

If I'd been wearing the dress shirt, I wouldn't have been in this position at all.

I reached an arm back to feel and cringed at the brush of my fingers across newly torn skin. When I brought my hand back, there was blood. Not too much, but enough. I twisted my neck again to look. Dammit, I needed a mirror.

I froze at the sound of the door as it squeaked open, my head angled over my shoulder. My breath sat trapped in my lungs until she slipped in, shutting the door behind her. Jolie. Kind eyes. Soft lips. My angel. My savior.

And the last person who should be here right now.

"You shouldn't be here." My voice was cautiously low, and despite my words, it was evident I was relieved to see her.

"Where else would I be, you moron? Turn around. Let me see."

I hesitated, not wanting her to see me like this—weak and wounded. She'd seen me like that so many times, I shouldn't have felt ashamed. And I didn't. Not really. Just.

I wanted to be different for her.

And as many times as I swore that I would be, her father still got the better of me.

"Come on, Cade," she said soothingly. "Let me."

Slowly, I turned, keeping my head craned so I could use her expression as a mirror. She barely flinched, but I saw it before her mask of compassion swallowed it up, and all I saw was love.

"It's not really that bad," she said.

"You're a bad liar." Actually, she was a good liar. I would have believed her if I couldn't feel the evidence to the contrary.

"I'm not lying. Most of them aren't even bleeding."

"Seriously? It feels like my whole back was torn open."

"I know." She tugged my T-shirt from my hands and patted it gently on a spot that must have been oozing.

I bit my cheek so I wouldn't cry like a big baby.

"They're really thin. Like cat scratches. I bet they don't even scar."

Probably why Headmaster Stark was so fond of the skinny-tailed whip. That and because it hurt the most.

I let my breath out slowly before attempting to speak. "That's not fair. I deserve a souvenir."

She forced a laugh and pulled a small tube from the pocket of her skirt. "You'll remember it. Trust me." She was still in her uniform, but her tie was loose, and even though class hours were over and we were no longer required to be in dress, I instinctively wanted her to fix it, just in case there was a chance she'd face the same punishment I'd faced.

Concern over her outfit got pushed away as she delicately rubbed the ointment along one of the stripes on my back.

"Holy fuck." So much for taking it like a man.

She winced. "I'm sorry. I don't want them to get infected."

It was hard to concentrate on words, the pain too blinding to think about much else. "Right. That's, um. Thanks. Good. Good thinking. Oh my fucking hell almighty Christ!"

"Shh." She was trying to be comforting but also reminding me to watch my volume.

It also reminded me of the risk she was taking just by being here. Tears pricked at the corners of my eyes, and I wasn't sure if they were from the pain or because she was helping me. There hadn't been much kindness in my world before her.

It was still hard to believe she was real. Hard to believe she was mine.

Of course, she was forbidden, so it wasn't like anyone knew she was mine. But she was all the same.

I blinked away the moisture in my eyes. I hadn't cried when I'd been beaten, I wasn't going to start now.

She finished applying the antibiotic and pressed her lips on one of the wounds, so gently that it barely stung. Then she snuck her arms around me, her hands moving low toward the crotch of my khaki uniform pants.

"Jolie," I warned. It would have been a perfect distraction from the agony of my wounds—her in my lap, my cock buried inside her, my kisses swallowing the sound of her moans.

But the risk...

"It would be worth it," she murmured, reading my mind.

I was hard when her hand cupped my bulge, but I put my palm over hers to stop her before we got carried away. Then I pulled her around to my front and settled my hands on her hips, holding her at arm's length. "We can't," I whispered sternly.

She glanced toward the door, seeming to assess the threat. Then she sighed. "I wish..."

"I know."

She looked up at me with yearning, the flecks of brown in her eyes more present at the moment than the green or the blue. She had kaleidoscope eyes, the colors always changing, and what I wouldn't give to spend hours lost inside her gaze, studying every shift of pigment. I wanted that even more than the hastily stolen moments we'd shared. Wanted to just be with her, seeing into her the way she always saw into me.

My resistance was weakening. I pressed my forehead against hers. "How can we live like this?"

"Like caged birds?" She brought her hands up to my cheeks, tilting my face so she could look at me directly. "It's not too hard if we just keep thinking that eventually we'll fly free. And we will, Cade. We won't be trapped like this forever."

I brushed my knuckles across her cheek. She had such delicate features, but in reality, she was so much stronger than me.

So much braver. Sometimes I swore she had courage enough for both of us.

I bent in to graze my lips against hers, but halted at a voice calling from outside the room. "Julianna?"

Her body tensed in recognition of her name. It was still far away though. She had time.

"Go," I said, ushering her toward the door. "Before he catches you here."

She took two steps away, then hurried back to press a fast kiss on my mouth and a half empty pack of cigarettes into my hand. "One day. We'll fly."

Then she was gone, out of the room before I could say anything else. I rushed after her and pressed my ear against the door, listening.

"In my office now, Julianna."

I couldn't tell if he was close enough to know where she'd just come from, or if he suspected. Her, "Yes, sir," gave nothing away.

My fingers curled into a fist at my side, ready to punch a hole in the wall, but I stopped myself, my wounds too fresh of a reminder about the consequences of rebellion.

I forced myself to take deep breaths instead, and held tight to the promise of *one day*.

FOUR

P *resent*

I SAT at Donovan's desk for a long time after Jolie left, my mind in a strange fog. There was so much new that I couldn't process, and I found myself back in the past.

We'd been so young. Made so many promises. I'd believed with every fiber of my being that she'd meant them at the time. So why hadn't she flown away with me?

It was a question I had never been able to answer, which was why I tended to avoid looking back at all costs.

Currently, the past felt surer than the present. I may have been wrong in the long run, but in that moment, when she'd risked everything to be at my side, I'd known what was between us. Known what we were. Known what I'd felt for her. Known I could trust her.

Now, I didn't know anything. I was blank. My body numb.

The only feeling I could identify was the decade-long forgotten urge for a smoke.

"I saw your lady friend leave a while ago and wondered if I'd missed you," a voice said.

The unexpected company snapped me out of my daze, and I looked up to find Fran standing in the doorway.

I must have been truly out of it. I hadn't even heard the elevator ding, let alone the clomp of her thick heels.

"Not so sure she's a lady. She's definitely not my friend." I stood and crossed to the closet, hidden in the bookshelves, and grabbed my coat. Now that I was in motion, I needed to stay in motion. "You good to lock up?"

"That's why I'm here."

"Thanks." I patted my coat pockets, as if I'd find a pack of cigarettes tucked away in one of them, an old reflex that had me cursing under my breath as soon as I realized it had kicked in. Then, ignoring the piece of paper with her phone number scrawled on it, I headed to the door, snagging one of Donovan's cigars on my way out. I wasn't much for the fancy shit he liked to puff on, but maybe it would satisfy the craving.

Once on the street, I realized I should have grabbed a lighter as well.

With another curse, I tucked the cigar in the breast pocket of my suit jacket and hailed a cab to the Park Hyatt. I'd missed the wedding ceremony at this point, but the reception would be going on for hours. Plus, I was staying at that hotel.

I considered bailing on the festivities altogether. Weston and I were both partners in the firm, but we weren't that buddy-buddy, and it was a fake wedding at that, some marriage-of-convenience scheme Donovan had concocted to help expand Reach in Europe. Honestly, business and money were probably the smartest reasons I could think of to get married, and in many ways I was more supportive of this union than most because of that. But since the parties involved considered it all for show, it wasn't like anyone would care if I ditched.

When I walked into the hotel lobby, though, I realized that if I didn't go to the reception, I'd end up at the bar. And ending up at the bar would be a sign that I wasn't okay, and I needed very much to be okay.

Another benefit of the reception? The booze was free.

Despite suggesting to Julianna that I'd dressed in my suit for the wedding, I'd actually rented a tux—or rather, Donovan had rented me a tuxedo. I'd found it waiting in my room when I'd checked in the day before. I was of half a mind to ignore the monkey suit and just go in what I was wearing. But I had my coat to deal with, and I didn't want to check it, so I headed up to my room to ditch it and ended up changing into the tux as well.

While I was up there, I lit the rich-ass cigar, ignoring the no-smoking sign blatantly posted in my suite with each puff. Serious cigar smokers don't inhale, but I sure as hell did, praying it would get me buzzed. The numbness was wearing off, and if I was going to feel, I wanted to be in control of what kind of feeling I had.

The cigar wasn't quite the fix I wanted, but I was a different kind of jittery when I found myself downstairs in the Onyx Ballroom—thank God for no line at the bar. The place was decked to the nines in luxury. Everything from the jazz band to the gift bags for the guests was Grade A wedding material, and even if the marriage hadn't been Grade A fake, I would have been nauseated at the sight.

A couple swigs into my beer and the urge to puke faded

away, as did the urge to smoke. The itchiness of the tux remained, but that had nothing to do with the event itself. Tuxes were always too constraining. I'd learned that the hard way when an art auction in Thailand had gone south. I'd left that situation with a busted kneecap and a bruised kidney that I was certain I could have prevented if my attire hadn't restricted movement. I'd hated the fancy-ass get-ups ever since.

At least Donovan had known well enough not to get me a cummerbund.

I did a quick scan of the room, looking for a familiar face, not expecting to find too many—the pompous wedding was mostly meant to appease the bride's family, so most of the guests were on her side. Plus, I hadn't been in New York in years, and I wasn't the type who had many connections to begin with. But it didn't take too long before I spotted Donovan with a hot brunette cozied up to him.

I paused a minute to take that in before approaching them. I'd known Donovan now going on seven years. In that time, I'd seen him with plenty of women—the man wasn't a whore, but he kept himself entertained. Never had any of those women been more than arm candy and (presumably) a good lay. He'd certainly never looked at anyone the way he was looking at this chick.

Of course, no chick had been *this* chick. He'd been carrying a torch for this one for the last decade. I didn't know a lot about her beyond a few drunken exchanges over the years, but I recognized in him what he probably recognized in me. There's a specific type of wariness in those who have loved and lost. Like speaks to like. We understood each other well.

But now the girl he'd pined for was in his arms, carrying the torch along with him.

And I was...

I wasn't going there, was where I was.

It took another swig of beer to loosen the tightness in my chest and another after that before I approached the couple. "Then the rumors are true," I said, startling them out of their embrace. "Donovan Kincaid has found himself a girlfriend."

Said girlfriend backed away from him as fast as a teenager caught making out by dad.

Maybe not *that* quickly. If anyone would know that panic, it was me.

"I'm the one who told you that rumor, you asshole," Donovan said, clapping his hand on my back.

He'd dropped it like a bomb, actually, when I'd called Tuesday to tell him I was coming to town. "*Great. You can meet our new director of marketing strategy. Oh, and by the way, she's my girlfriend.*"

Unable to get more from him, I'd asked Weston about it when I'd called with my late wedding RSVP. He'd filled me in with as much as he knew, which wasn't a hell of a lot that was meaningful. He had more to say about his own tryst with the woman than Donovan's relationship with her. Too much to say about her, really. I hadn't needed the intimate details. But that was to be expected—Weston liked to gloat about his conquests, and Donovan was tight-lipped.

Truth was, I hadn't needed to hear anything from either of them to put together that this girlfriend was *the* girlfriend. The fact that Donovan had abandoned me in Tokyo and moved back to the States as soon as this woman from the past was hired told me everything I needed to know.

"Sabrina, this is Cade Warren," Donovan said, making the official introduction. "Cade, I told you about Sabrina."

It was possible he was hinting for me to play that up, make the girlfriend feel all warm and fuzzy because her boyfriend had been talking about her. If he was, well, he had to know me better than that. "No. *You* told me about our new director of marketing strategy. Weston told me about Sabrina."

I shook her hand, taking in her features as I did. Big brown doe eyes, rail thin frame. The kind of beautiful that turned heads. No wonder the boys had both been into her. "Pleasure to meet you. Everything I've heard has been quite...complimentary."

I was a little more friendly with her than necessary, forcing myself to be present for reasons beyond seeing if it would rile Donovan up.

Apparently it did. "Cade's story that he's here for the wedding is only a cover," he said pointedly. "He's really in the States to meet up with a woman from the past."

I narrowed my eyes. "Hey—"

"Payback's a bitch." He wrapped his arm around Sabrina's waist and pulled her closer like he owned her, which knowing him, he probably thought he did.

"That was supposed to be a secret." I made sure my tone reminded him that I was still someone to be afraid of. In case he'd forgotten that I hadn't been innocent when he'd met me. He knew the kinds of things I could do to people. The kinds of things I'd done.

Not murder, though. I'd never gone that far.

Could I go that far? Would I, if...?

"Sabrina and I have no secrets," Donovan said, and as soft as it made him sound, I had the gut feeling that *he* would kill if he had to. For her.

But I wasn't Donovan. And Jolie wasn't in my arms. And I sure as fuck wasn't killing anyone for her.

And even if, once upon a time, I was the type of guy who would have killed for her, this share-all-my-secrets-pussy-whipped bullshit was not ever going to be my scene.

I rolled my eyes. "Well, isn't that precious?"

"Don't worry. Your secret is safe with me." At least Sabrina seemed to understand I was a man not to reckon with.

Though, I wasn't sure it was that important to keep the meeting with Julianna on the down low. At first, I hadn't wanted people to know because who would understand besides Donovan? Now that I knew what she'd wanted from me, it was a different story. If I were going to help her, any communication with her could incriminate me.

I wasn't going to help her, obviously. But if she went through with it herself and someone later had questions for me...Yeah, that was a whole can of worms I didn't want to get involved with. Best to keep it hush.

I needed to clue Donovan in on that so he wouldn't mouth off to anyone else, and I planned to do that as soon as I had the chance. With how tightly he gripped his "girlfriend," and the office staff now gathered around us, it wasn't going to be anytime soon.

Good thing I had my beer.

FIVE

Another twenty minutes of chitchat and mingling with staff, and I was beyond ready to get the fuck out of that ballroom. Free booze or no, the lovey-dovey vibe had me twitchy as shit. Although I'd met most of the employees at one time or another, I hadn't worked with any of them enough to be able to hold a meaningful conversation, and I was...distracted.

Distracted by light eyes and womanly curves and dyed blonde hair that somehow looked more natural than the brown I'd been used to imagining. Distracted by a request that I could never take seriously and the secretive reasons behind the request and the goddamned proof that the woman I'd once loved still existed in this world.

So much for fucking closure.

I needed to be drunk. And for as drunk as I planned to be, I was going to need to eat something more substantial than the fancy hors d'oeuvres the caterers were serving. Time to think about getting out of there.

The universe rarely worked in my favor, but just then the speaker system announced Mr. and Mrs. Weston and Elizabeth King, and finally—since I'd been informed by Donovan that I had to wait until they'd arrived to take off—I was closer to escape. Hallelujah.

"They do a lineup or something, don't they?" I finished my beer with one long swallow. Maybe I could rush through it, give my congrats, and let them know the gift was in the mail (then remember to call my assistant and make sure she'd sent something in my name).

I'd meant the question for Donovan, but it was Roxie, Weston's secretary, who answered. "I think they plan to mingle."

For the first time since I'd arrived, I sized up the crowd. Jesus, the place was packed. There were already several small bunches gathered near the bride and groom, people waiting for their turn to coo over the couple. The rest of the afternoon would be like this, Weston and his new wife the center of attention while they cut the cake and did the dance and threw the garter. Were they doing all that traditional bullshit?

Another unbidden memory popped in my head. Jolie in my arms, her cheek pressed to my chest. *"We can't have a wedding,"* I'd told her, and I remembered feeling disappointed by that. *"We'll have to elope. There won't be a big ceremony. No reception. None of it."*

"I don't care about that. All I care about is being with you."

I shook the memory from my thoughts, but the essence of it lingered like a bad scent after the garbage had been taken out. "Fuck this. It will take forever for them to get through all these people. I'm taking off."

I tossed my bottle into a nearby trash can, then crossed to

my business partner, interrupting another session of canoodling with a tap on his shoulder. "Can I borrow you for a moment, Donovan?" I forced myself to acknowledge his woman, even though all I wanted to do was get some place that didn't feel so claustrophobic. Some place I could breathe. "It was nice meeting you, Sabrina. I'll probably see you around the office before I head back to Tokyo."

She said, "Ditto," but I was already walking away, Donovan in tow.

"I want to hear this," he said when he caught up to me, "but make it quick."

Not even two seconds away from his girl, and he was already on edge. "You're so fucking pussy whipped."

"You want to know something, Cade?" When I turned my head toward him, he flipped me the bird.

Neither of us spoke again until we were outside the ballroom in the lounge. It wasn't as empty as I would have preferred, but it would do for the conversation I needed to have now. The rest could wait. "You didn't tell anyone else why I was in town, right?"

"You mean that you were in town for Weston's wedding? I told the whole goddamn office because, as you seem to have correctly assumed, I talk about you nonstop."

I gave him an impatient glare. I wasn't in the mood for his sarcasm.

He returned the glare with his who-do-you-think-I-am look. "I didn't tell anyone, you moron."

"Except Sabrina."

He didn't roll his eyes, but his expression had the same effect. "Except Sabrina, and you were right there in the room when it happened."

"Good, good." I'd thought the confirmation would calm me, but my shoulders felt just as tightly drawn as before. "You're sure she won't tell anyone?"

"She won't."

"You'll make sure?"

"I'll make sure. What the hell happened when you saw her?"

He would have wanted to know no matter what, but after my paranoid interrogation, he had to be even more piqued. For as much as the asshole had done for me, he did deserve an explanation.

I glanced around the space. "Not here."

Donovan gestured to a room nearby, the door slightly open. "The bride used it to get ready. Bet it's empty now."

If I got started, I wasn't going to stop. I'd need copious amounts of liquor for that, and I doubted the dressing room had a suitable minibar. Besides, Donovan had already spelled out his desired time frame for this interaction.

"I'll fill you in later. When we're somewhere else."

He narrowed his eyes, reluctant to let it drop. "She showed, though?"

I nodded and did another scan of the lounge. Experience and necessity had turned me into a vigilant man, but I recognized I was probably being overly cautious. Talking about her always felt unsafe, not just today. She'd been my secret too long for me to feel any other way about her.

But now she didn't need to be my anything. I'd seen her, and I could stop looking for her and move on. "You can take that PI of yours off the job."

"You don't want him to do any more digging? He was waiting for her after your meeting. I'm sure he's got more—"

"No. Call him off." I wasn't even sure why I'd had the guy look in the first place. Years of coming up with nothing had only driven my curiosity to keep searching.

"Did you get a phone number, at least? My guy could probably get you a whole background from that, as long as it's not a burner phone."

I thought briefly about the note she'd written, still sitting on Donovan's desk. I should have torn it up and thrown it away. I should have destroyed it.

Because right now that simple sheet of paper called to me like a siren song, begging me to return so it could destroy *me*.

"I don't care anymore." I told myself I meant it.

"You're sweating and twitchy and smell like one of my Fuentes—you're welcome, by the way. You'd never reach voluntarily for a cigar unless you were worked up. That doesn't seem like a man who doesn't care."

Reading between the lines was Donovan's superpower. Normally, it was something I admired. Today, his perception made me want to snap. "I don't care about her," I reiterated with finality.

"Whatever you say."

Hearing myself, I wouldn't buy it either. "Just cancel the PI, okay? And don't tell anyone about me seeing her. Not Weston, not Nate—no one. I mean it."

"Okay." He studied me for several seconds. "Something big happened, didn't it?"

Even without her insane—not to mention illegal—request, "big" was an understatement. I hadn't had time to process it yet, hadn't let myself begin. The numbness had completely worn off, though, and in its place was a tar pit of emotion. As soon as I started walking through it, I knew I was going to be stuck.

Stuck was where I'd been for years. Was I really just right back where I started?

"I'll tell you about it tomorrow," I assured him. "All of it."

"Stop by my place in the afternoon."

"Fine." Without a goodbye, I spun away from him. I'd spent as much energy on him as I could. The rest I needed to keep myself from falling apart.

"Cade," he called after me.

It took more strength to turn and listen than to keep going, but I forced myself to stop all the same. "What?"

"Don't do anything stupid."

It was hard not to laugh at the late warning. She'd reached out, and I'd come running. What could be more stupid than that?

SIX

"Re-al li-fe," the girl said slowly, her head tilted to read the letters spelled out across the back of my fingers. "Real life."

"Yep. Real life."

"It's a bitch sometimes," she said with a wink.

My chuckle disappeared behind a swig of bourbon. What did she know about it? She was only twenty-two according to the bartender's pronouncement. He'd read it out loud when she'd handed her ID over the first time, and he'd been the one to wink when he'd passed it back. He made no bones about his intent to seduce her, hinting more than once that his shift was over in an hour. He probably wasn't much older than she was.

I, on the other hand, had thirteen years on her, which meant she was at least three years too young, and that was definitely one of the reasons she was coming back to my room with *me*. She had bad decision written all over her, and that couldn't have been a better match for my mood.

Tough luck, my bartender friend. I'd leave him a big tip to make up for stealing his conquest.

"Do your tattoos go all the way up?" the girl asked now, fondling my arm.

"What do you think?" My bicep flexed instinctively under her hand, and she practically purred.

I'd probably get her to meow when we were both naked. If she wasn't too drunk.

If *I* wasn't too drunk.

And fuck. I was headed for too drunk if I wasn't there already.

"Hmm. I have a guess. Maybe I'll get to find out if I'm right." She ran her hand down my sleeve before dropping it to pick up her cosmo. I still wore the tux jacket, but I'd managed to lose the stupid bowtie—and by lose, I meant cutie pie next to me had it wrapped around her neck like a choker. It gave her a sexy playgirl look that had my cock interested, even if the rest of me was somewhat numb to her charm, but that was the way with most of my encounters with women. It was the head in my pants that did the scoping out and drove the pickups. Generally, he liked the ones that didn't talk so much. The ones that didn't giggle. This chick was out of the norm because she did both, but he perked up whenever she tossed her hair over her shoulder, which was quite often.

Seemed we liked blondes now. That was new.

"I wonder if blondes really do have more fun."

The memory stormed in without warning—Jolie standing in front of a mirror, holding her hair up with one hand. A fingerprint-shaped bruise on her neck that made me want to ask questions that I didn't need to ask.

"Don't even think it. I like it dark," I'd said. But I'd been

focused on that bruise, not her hair, and even though I knew it wasn't worth getting her upset, I had a sick impulse to hear about every pain that monster inflicted on her. If she had to suffer it, I needed to suffer it too.

"Like I'd ever get away with it. Just let me dream for a minute."

I'd reached my hand out to press gently against the marked skin, erasing her smile from her face. She dropped her hair and put her hand on my wrist. *"Let it go, Cade."*

"I need to know."

"You already know."

I'd bit my cheek until it bled, the familiar coppery taste reminding me that I hated telling her about my bruises too.

With a sigh, I'd let my hand fall. *"You should dye it as soon as we leave."* I didn't believe blondes really had more fun, but I'd figured she deserved every chance at happiness she could get.

And now Jolie was away from her father, and her hair was lighter like she'd wanted, and I hadn't seen any bruises, but if she was anything like me, she still wore them under her skin. My insides were even more marked up than my outsides.

That wasn't something I planned on sharing with a girl I'd just met in a bar.

Forcing my attention back to her—the current blonde at my side—I turned in, and the jostle of someone stepping up to the bar behind me gave an excuse to step an inch closer, staking claim. "Do you have any?"

"Have any what?" She blinked up at me, her eyes glossy, and it occurred to me she was on her way to too drunk too, which was fine. It would make it a fairer coupling.

"Tats."

"Oh! Tattoos! Yes."

I wasn't really precious about my own ink. Only a couple held any meaning. The rest were acquired to help create an image—*respect* written on my forearm, *beast* down my bicep, the cross-shaped dagger on my hand. Looking tough had been an essential part of my former job. It was a wonder Donovan had seen past it, but I was lucky he had. My current career was more satisfying, not to mention safer. Oh, and one hundred percent legal.

Though no longer necessary for work, I'd learned that talking about tats was a handy topic for hookups. "Where they at?" After a second, I added, "The tats," in case she'd already forgotten again.

"I have a butterfly across the top of my foot. It hurt so bad I'm scared of getting another."

"Because it's near the bone." The bartender set another cosmo in front of her. "On the house." Either he'd missed my stake and was clueless or he was cocky enough to not care.

"Next time get one where there's lots of flesh." My innuendo was as much for her as for the bartender, to let him know he wasn't the only one seducing.

"It hurts less on the fleshy parts?" Another toss of her hair. Another twitch of my dick.

"Presumably."

"You'll have to show me a good spot, then, Cade."

She got points for remembering my name. I didn't remember hers, and wouldn't if she repeated it, so I didn't bother asking. It had been years since I remembered any name besides Jolie. Not likely I'd start now.

"The tat on the outside of my arm wasn't bothersome." The bartender busied himself with wiping down the counter, an obvious excuse to keep talking to Blondie. "Inside hurt a bit more."

Blondie considered. "I don't think I'd get a tattoo on my arm."

"Mine wasn't too bad," a voice came from behind me. A woman inserting herself into a flirty conversation meant one of two things to my drunken brain—either she was hitting on the bartender, or she was hitting on me.

I supposed it was possible she was hitting on Blondie. I was already thinking threesome as I turned to include her in the conversation, my mouth opened to spout off some provocative quip.

It shut without a word uttered when I realized the other woman was Jolie.

Not Jolie. Julianna.

Too late, I realized her voice had been familiar. If I'd been sober, I would have placed it sooner, and what would that have gained me? Because whether I recognized it sooner or not, she'd still be here, and I'd still be speechless, and drunk as I was, I wasn't drunk enough to not have feelings about that.

What those feelings were was harder to identify.

"Where is it?" Blondie asked across me, her world continuing to spin while mine had stopped.

"My right hip," Julianna answered.

"And you said it didn't hurt?"

"Not any more than a bee sting."

"Bee stings hurt." The girl pouted.

I took another swig of my bourbon. Then another. Hoping each swallow would settle the thump of my heart. Each swallow failing.

She'd tracked me down. Of course she had. I hadn't said

whose wedding I was here for, but it wouldn't have been too hard to figure out since Weston's was publicized heavily. A simple Google search for Reach would have probably brought it up. That had to be how she found me.

I couldn't decide how I felt about the fact that she'd been looking.

"And what are you having, pretty thing?"

I should have been glad that the bartender now had his sights fixed on Jo—on Julianna, but for some reason it just made me want to punch a hole through the counter. Or through his face.

"Martini. In and out with the vermouth." She handed over her ID when he asked for it with a roll of her eyes. "You probably want me to take that as a compliment, but all I see it as is a hassle."

His expression went cold. "Just following the law, ma'am."

"Well, follow it with a little less smarm, will you?"

Yeah, that hookup wasn't happening. Fuck me for almost smiling.

Another swallow. Of all the gin joints, in all the world...

"Did yours hurt?" The slight pressure of Blondie's hand back on my forearm drew my attention back to her.

That's it. Focus on her. But her question didn't make sense in my stupor. *Did it hurt?* Yes, goddammit, it hurt. After all these years, after all the booze, it still fucking hurt, and it wasn't fucking fair.

"Your tattoos," she clarified. She placed her palm over the back of my hand and laced her fingers through mine. "Lots of bone here. Did it hurt?"

My dick didn't even register her touch, but I flirted back,

interested now in the hookup to prove something rather than to get off. "I'm a man. Which means I was crying like a baby."

She laughed. "No, you weren't."

"No, I wasn't." Each time I'd sat under the needle, I'd welcomed the pain, curious to see if this time I'd feel something new.

But the only thing I ever felt was the same old constant ache. It never varied. Never dulled. I'd carried it so long now, it was as much a part of me as any ink on my skin. I barely noticed it these days.

With *her* back in my life, sitting close enough that her arm brushed against mine, that ache burned as though it were new.

I turned my hand over so that Blondie and I were now palm to palm and imagined the dagger drawn on the back plunging through the heart of the woman on my other side. If only it had the power—if only *I* had the power to inflict pain on her.

I didn't believe for a minute that I did, but it felt damn good to pretend.

Blondie moved close enough that her breasts pressed against my bicep. "What other tattoos do you have?"

"That's the kind of question better answered with my clothes off."

"But the tux makes them look so hot."

"They're just as hot without. Trust me." I hadn't reached the level of drunk that I'd been aiming for, but it was about time to take this to my suite. The only thing keeping me was wanting a reaction from the woman next to me. She might not be at all bothered by me slutting it up in front of her, but she had to be irritated that I'd barely spared her a glance. She'd come looking for me. She at least wanted my attention.

The bartender returned with the martini. "Charge it to your room?"

I held my breath waiting for Julianna's answer, praying she hadn't gone so far as to book herself in the Park Hyatt. When she threw down a twenty, I was surprised to not feel more relief.

"What's yours?" Blondie asked the bartender. "You said it was on your arm?"

I guess we were still talking about tats.

"Tribal design. It goes all across here." He gestured with his hand, indicating he had a half sleeve.

Tribal design. If I weren't so intoxicated, I'd kick his ass just for being predictable.

But since I was intoxicated, and because I was obsessed and had been for years, I suddenly couldn't think about anything other than the flesh above Julianna's hip.

"What's yours?" I asked, the question out before I could stop myself.

If she was surprised I'd spoken to her, she didn't show it. "That's the kind of question better answered with my clothes off."

Direct hit.

Fuck her for landing it.

Fuck her for making me steal a glance at her, and fuck my head for the split second of thinking about her naked.

Remembering her naked.

I finished off my bourbon, then pushed the glass toward the bartender. "Another."

So much for taking off soon.

SEVEN

At the realization that there would be at least one more drink before the action started, Blondie leaned in to whisper in my ear. "I'll be back. I need to head to the ladies'."

I smiled like she'd said something dirty. Then, before she'd walked too far away, I pulled her back and kissed her. PDA wasn't generally my M.O. Frankly, neither was kissing. I preferred to have as little of it as possible when I fucked.

But this kiss was about making a point—the point that I was fine and desirable and not affected.

I didn't know if I was making that point for Jolie or for me.

Blondie was breathless by the time I let her go, at any rate. My breathing had been erratic before our lips locked and had nothing to do with her. I didn't even watch her walk away, when normally, if the woman from my past hadn't shown up, I would have followed after for a quickie in the restroom.

It was a couple tense seconds later that I realized that my much needed distraction had just walked away.

I chugged down half the glass of bourbon the minute the bartender set it down.

Maybe she'd leave.

Maybe she wouldn't say anything.

Maybe she...

"She's right," she said. "The tats are potently sexy combined with the tux."

I told myself not to engage.

I didn't listen. "I suppose that's why I chose to wear it."

"To show off your tats?"

"Yep." Short. Clipped. The message clear: this conversation was done. She and I were done.

"That's a lot of fuss to show off a bit of color. And you can't really see anything besides the ink on your hands—I'm assuming you have more underneath. You'd think you'd wear something that you could roll up. Show off the art on your arms or your chest. More likely, I'd say you probably wore the tux for some other reason. A wedding perhaps?"

I felt tense all over, pissed off that she thought we could sit here and chat like there was nothing between us. Like we were strangers who'd just met at the bar.

I dared another glance, allowing myself to check her out like she was just that—a stranger that I'd never seen before. She wore a black, spaghetti-strap dress with a slit up the thigh, the material sheer enough that I could see a hint of areola.

Shit, she was hot.

Not just woman-I've-been-fantasizing-about-for-eons hot, but grab-every-dick-in-the-rooms-attention hot. If she'd been a stranger who'd popped up at the bar—and if she hadn't been interested in a threesome—I would have dumped Blondie for her.

I probably would have dumped the idea of a threesome no matter what. Stranger in black made it impossible to see anyone but her once I was looking.

What could have happened between us if this was when and how we'd met? No doubt I would have asked her to my room. Would she have come?

Maybe because I was drunk or because I was fucked in the head or because there were parts of me that had longed to be in her presence for too long to walk away without more words exchanged, whatever the reason, I found myself turning toward her. Found myself putting on the charm. Found myself dipping a toe into the stranger fantasy. "I'd never let an event dictate my dress code."

"You dress for the ladies," she said smoothly, as though we'd both been playing the fantasy all along.

In a way, we had been. We were more strangers than anything else after all these years. It really didn't take much pretending. "Definitely for the ladies. This look is a chick magnet."

"Does it really work?"

"Seems to be working just fine." I waited for her to protest, to say that she wasn't drawn to me. Dared her with my stare to say it.

She didn't blink, but her eyes drifted toward the exit where Blondie had disappeared a few minutes before. "I think that one's drunk enough to not care what you're wearing."

"Is that a judgment?" I wanted it to be jealousy.

She hesitated before grinning. "It's an observation."

"You hand out observations to all the men you happen upon at bars?"

"If they're hot." Blondie had already referred to me as such tonight, yet it felt like it was the first time I'd ever heard it. "If it will start a conversation."

"Judgy observations are an obnoxious way to get noticed. I'd recommend another tactic."

"I don't know. Seems to be working just fine." She smiled smugly this time, and I couldn't help returning it. Her eyes had lit up, and it was even easier to look at her than it had been, and it had been very easy before.

The banter was easy as well. Too easy. We could anticipate each other's rhythm. There was no learning curve, just a fall into familiar patterns. If she were fishing in this pond, I'd already be in her bucket.

I wasn't sure if she *was* fishing. There was every chance she wanted to forget our past as much as I did, that she also sought closure. Leave it to her to go for the hot, sweaty ending. There might be benefits to fucking her out of my system. I could do that. All night long, if that's what it took.

It was more likely she was only trying to seduce me into helping her deal with her daddy issue.

I took a sip of my drink, rerouting my thoughts. Reminding myself she was a stranger. "So you have the conversation started. Are you as good at keeping it going?"

"I tend to find that starting is all I really need. After that, who needs talk?"

She did this too well—the stranger game. The seduction. I wondered how often she did this sort of thing and hated myself for wanting to know all the names and details of every man she'd ever hit on, ever sucked off, ever let inside her, just so I could track them down and bash each and every one of their heads into the ground.

I would not kill for her. Not even in a jealous rage. Not even just in my head.

"Pro at pickups, are you?" My tone was cool.

"Never said that."

"You don't have to."

"Really? Now who's making judgments?"

"Just observing, baby. Just observing." I was such a liar. I was all judgment and jealousy, and even if I could successfully compartmentalize and separate the woman in front of me from the one from the past—from the one even this morning—that only worked for my head. These emotions were too primitive for reason.

Still, I couldn't tear myself away. "What about you? Why do you look so..." *Sexy, spectacular, devastating.* "Fancy?"

She looked down at her outfit as if she'd forgotten what she put on. "Not sure a basic black dress counts as fancy."

"Huh. Just a basic black dress." Now who was lying? That dress was anything but basic. That dress was a well-chosen weapon.

But she kept up the ruse. "Heels and red lipstick. It's a magic trick."

My eyes had a mind of their own, wandering down to where her steepled nipples pressed the fabric away from her body. God, in the right light, that dress was obscene. Made me want to do obscene things. "You use the magic trick for yourself or for someone else?"

"I was hoping to run into someone."

"Then I'm getting in the way." But I took a step closer.

"You aren't getting in the way at all."

For a handful of seconds I really considered it. Considered forgetting that I was the someone she'd been hoping to run into.

Considered really letting myself be someone different. Considered slipping my arm around her waist and escorting her to my room for a night with no names and no strings and no baggage.

But she'd expect there to be strings in the morning.

And the baggage was sewn into me.

And I knew her name better than I knew my own.

I shot back the rest of my drink and slammed the empty glass on the bar so hard that eyes turned in our direction. I ignored them as I lay into her. "Why don't you go by Julianna anymore?"

There was a lot to be angry about when it came to her. Her name was only the first one to make it to the tip of my tongue, probably because it was the latest of the hurts she'd doled out over our lifetime, salt on a wound that would never ever heal.

Her face fell, but she quickly recovered, and now she was the woman she'd been in the office. Softer. Provocative, but only because she couldn't not be rather when seconds before it had been on purpose. "Julianna isn't who I wanted to be."

"But that's who you chose to be."

"I didn't choose anything," she snapped, as if I didn't know anything about her.

"Didn't you?" My voice was a blade. "You had the chance to be Jolie. You didn't take it."

"I know."

"You don't get to pretend everything is water under the bridge."

She looked guiltier with this. "I know."

Her acknowledgments weren't satisfying. Not when I wanted to fight. "You don't get to pop up suddenly and try to tell me that's who you are now."

"But it is," she said, her blue-green eyes flashing. "It's who I've always been. Since you gave me that name."

Now it was her with the blade, its tip held at my gut as she tried to tell me that Jolie had existed all these years without me. Trying to tell me that there was a very real part of her that was still mine.

I wouldn't hear it. Couldn't. "That girl is gone. Honestly? I'm not sure she ever really existed."

Without giving her a chance to say anything else, I pushed away from the bar and crossed the lounge to meet Blondie returning from the restroom. "Let's get out of here, baby," I said.

"Mm. Yes."

I grabbed her ass, glancing over my shoulder to be sure blue-green eyes were watching as I steered her toward the elevator. I could still spend tonight fucking Jolie out of my system.

I'd just do it fucking some other girl.

EIGHT

I woke up with regrets.

My neck ached from my awkward sleeping position. For some crazy reason, I'd decided to pass out on the couch. The hangover wasn't too bad, at least. I knew well enough how to handle my liquor and had made sure I was plenty hydrated before I crashed.

Nevertheless, my mouth tasted like shame, and my body ached with remorse.

I shouldn't have gone to the bar. I should have drunk myself into a stupor in the safety of my room. I shouldn't have been somewhere that I could be found.

I shouldn't have come to New York in the first place.

Movement from the suite's bedroom reminded me why I'd ended up out here.

"You're awake," Blondie said, walking out with the sheet wrapped around her body, mascara streaked and her eyes bleary.

I'd forgotten about her.

I'd forgotten about her when I was with her, to be honest. She was naked underneath that sheet, and I was fully aware I'd been the one who'd gotten her that way, but she hadn't been who I'd been thinking about when I did. The woman I'd pictured underneath me had slightly smaller tits and specks of green in her blue eyes and a gaze that saw right into me.

Yeah, I was a real piece of trash.

I scrubbed my hand over my face. "Yeah. I'm awake."

"Sorry again about putting you out of a bed. You could have slept with me." She was bashful with her flirting, not like she was trying to be coy, but like she was nervous about the morning-after routine.

I wasn't used to it myself. Generally, I was the asshole who made them go when the performance was through. Blondie was only here because she'd left her purse with her ID, phone, and room key at the bar, and by the time we'd gotten around to noticing, the place was closed up for the night. Since the front desk wouldn't give her another room key without identification, I'd let her stay.

Guess I wasn't a *complete* asshole.

"I don't sleep well with others," I told her, which was what I'd said last night as well as the truth. "It's a me thing, not you."

She scanned the room, as though it was easier to look anywhere but directly at me. "Well. The restaurant should be open now. I'll get dressed and get out of your hair."

She was hoping the purse had been tucked away in the restaurant safe rather than stolen, counting on it even since she refused use of my laptop when I offered so she could put a stop on her credit card.

I didn't have quite such an optimistic outlook on humanity.

"If you wait until I get some things together, I'll go down with you in case it's not there."

I wasn't sure what I'd offer to her if it wasn't. I wasn't going to leave her completely stranded, but I was also long past ready for her to be out of my hair.

She shut the door to get changed, even though I'd seen everything, and I was grateful. If she'd left it open, it would have been an invitation, and I didn't want to deal with hurt feelings when I turned it down. I wasn't a fuck-every-chance-you-get kind of guy like Weston was. I had to be in the mood for sex, and for the most part, that mood only struck when I was lonely and liquored up.

Or, apparently, when I was trying to distract myself from someone else.

Shaking off thoughts of *her*, I pulled on the jeans and sweater I'd brought out from the bedroom the night before. Then I went to the closet by the front door to grab my duffel bag with gym clothes. There was a fitness center in the hotel, but I needed more than a treadmill and rowing machine. Fortunately, I'd located a boxing club a couple blocks away when I'd made my reservation, and I'd come prepared, suspecting I'd need to burn some energy off on this trip.

By the time Blondie came back out, I had my shoes and coat on, ready to go. She'd scrubbed her face and pulled her hair back into a bun held with the complimentary hotel pen and didn't look like a woman who had partied too hard. Even so, the dress from last night was too much bling for daywear, making her walk of shame obvious.

I considered loaning her my coat, but I needed my coat, and I didn't owe her anything, so I didn't feel too bad about not making the offer. With a nod, I gestured to the door and followed her out. Thankfully, she didn't attempt to make small talk, and we managed to get in the elevator and travel to the lobby floor in silence.

There was a group of people waiting for the elevator when the doors opened. I put a gentlemanly hand at Blondie's back to steer her around them, and so that's how we were when Jolie saw us.

Actually, I saw her first, which was why I didn't drop my hand immediately.

She was impossible to miss, her voice raised as she argued with the front desk clerk. "No, it's not fine. I need the room until Friday."

I couldn't hear the clerk's response. I wasn't sure she heard it either because that was the moment she looked up and saw me, my arm around the woman from the night before, and for a full second I gloated. How many times had I wished for exactly that scenario? To bump into Jolie with a younger, prettier woman on my arm. To show her I was doing better than fine and she could eat her heart out.

It only lasted that second, though, before it fizzled into misery. Blondie wasn't prettier by a long shot, and even if she were, she didn't mean anything to me, and I wasn't doing fine, and it was highly unlikely Jolie would ever eat her heart out over me. That was me that did that. That was still doing it.

I dropped my hand, and Jolie turned her focus back to the clerk. Her voice softer now, but still discernible. "Could you try it again? I know you already did, but just once more?"

It wasn't my business. Whatever she was fussing about, I wasn't part of it. I needed to keep walking.

"Hey, uh." I stumbled since I didn't have a name to end the

statement with. "How about you go on ahead? I'm going to be..." I nodded at the desk. At Jolie.

"Oh, the woman from last night!" She surveyed the situation, quickly catching on. "You gonna rescue her? Look at you being everyone's knight in shining armor."

I cringed. I was not a hero. I was definitely not Jolie's hero.

What I was, apparently, was a masochist, because I kept finding myself drawn to the woman who had become synonymous with pain. "Let me know if you don't find your purse," I said dismissively.

Jolie had angled her body after spotting me so she didn't notice me come up until I was already there. "What seems to be the trouble?" I did that douchebag man thing where I addressed the clerk instead of her. To be fair, it wasn't because she was a woman—it was because she was her.

"It's nothing, Cade. A problem with my card." Jolie dismissed me without even looking at me.

She wanted me gone, and for some fucked-up reason, that was exactly the reason why I stayed.

NINE

"I've tried three times," the clerk said patiently, handing the credit card back to Jolie. "It's still showing..." He lowered his voice, trying to be discreet. "Declined."

Her cheeks flushed, but her expression stayed cool. She took the card back and pulled another from the wallet open on the counter in front of her. "Please, can you run this one instead?"

"Yes, Ms.—"

She cut him off sharply. "It's Jolie. Please."

"I'll try it right now, Jolie."

"Thank you." I could feel her vibrating with anxiety as the clerk ran the card through the reader.

I stepped closer, needing to soak up her energy. Not because I thought I could take it from her or because I liked negative emotions, but because it was palpable and hers, and I'd spent so many years yearning to be close enough to her to know what she was feeling that I couldn't help being drawn into it now.

Her eyes flicked to me, then back to the clerk. "Go away, Cade."

I didn't move. The clerk, on the other hand, looked up, assessing the situation, probably trying to decide if he should interfere with whatever was going on between the guests standing in front of him.

After a beat, he smiled brightly. "Give me a moment. It might be the machine. Let me try another."

Without waiting for a response, he took Jolie's credit card and disappeared into the back room under the pretenses of trying to run it again. I strongly suspected he was giving us time to resolve our altercation on our own so he wouldn't have to deal with me. People often found me intimidating like that.

As soon as he was gone, I turned to Jolie. "Are you strapped—"

She wouldn't let me even finish the sentence. "This isn't your problem. You don't need to get involved."

It was a little nervy for her to push my help away a day after she'd come begging for it. "Little late for that, don't you think?"

"No, I don't think. You made it blatantly clear that you had no interest."

It didn't matter that she was speaking fact. Being dismissed pissed me off all the same. Unreasonably. I huffed, trying to come up with some pointed comeback when I caught the eye of Blondie returning from the bar. She held her purse up for me to see and gave me a wave.

At least that was resolved. I'd have my suite back to myself.

When I waved back, Jolie followed my eyeline to see Blondie scurrying to the elevator.

"Is she your girlfriend?" Her voice was even tighter than before.

I considered for a moment, trying to decide if I wanted to answer what Jolie had asked or give her the answer I was sure she wanted. "Not really," I said, not feeling generous enough to tell her I didn't do girlfriends.

She rolled her eyes. "Oh, one of those." I didn't get a chance to drill her on her meaning before she asked, "What's her name?"

"Cassie," I said, thinking quickly.

"Weird that her purse has Addie stitched across it."

I squinted toward my one-night stand waiting for the elevator. "You couldn't see that from here."

"I saw it last night."

Cassie/Addie. Close enough. More importantly... "If you already knew her name, why did you ask?"

"I wanted to see if you knew it." The triumphant look on her face was so familiar, reminding me how she always loved to be right, and how she loved to revel in her victory, and how I loved to kiss that look right off of her lips.

Her lips were just as plump and tempting as they'd been back then.

Fuck her and her lips and her trap to one-up me. "Seems weird that you noticed her purse."

She turned away from me, facing straight ahead, her triumph tempered with a mask of disinterest that she couldn't quite pull off. "Why? Girls notice each other's things."

"In my experience, they only notice when they're being catty." I was pulling shit from my ass, but I liked how it sounded. "Why would you be spiteful to a girl you just met? Are you jealous?"

Her head turned toward me so fast, her hair swung. "Jealous?! You've got to be kidding me."

I hadn't believed it when I said it. I was just trying to poke her a bit because I resented her and enjoyed seeing her provoked.

But the way she reacted—her face red, her eyes blazing—I almost wondered if there was something to it.

No way I wasn't leaning into that. "I think it's a reasonable enough question. Can't figure why else you'd care. And your reaction now confirms it."

"There was no reaction. I was curious. Politely curious. And now I'm—"

The clerk returned, and her expression quickly shifted to something friendlier. "Did it work?"

Her tone said she knew it hadn't gone through before the guy answered. "I was able to get your current room charge to go through, but it won't accept the prepayment for the rest of your stay."

Two credit cards with no credit available.

"You don't have money?" It came out like an accusation. I hadn't meant that exactly. I was more just...surprised. I had a real nice bank account now, but when I'd known her, she'd been the one with money. Her father, anyway. A decent amount, too. The kind of amount that made him look noble for continuing to headmaster the school that had been in his family for generations instead of hiring someone else to do it. The kind of money that would not be used up before he died.

So why the hell was Old Man Stark not taking care of the daughter he'd always been so protective of?

Things were beginning to click. "Is that why...? Because you need his—"

"I don't want to discuss this here," she snapped. "Please."

Fair enough.

"We're going to get the bill covered," I said to the clerk, ignoring Jolie's attempt to disagree. "We just need a moment to discuss the finances. Be right back. I'm leaving this for insurance." I didn't know if he actually needed insurance, but I dropped my duffel bag on the counter all the same.

"All right. Sure." The clerk appeared relieved to see us go as I grabbed Jolie's elbow and pulled her with me down the hall, trying the handles of closed doors, searching for one that would open to someplace private where I could drill her more thoroughly.

She fought me verbally the entire way. "Where are you taking me? Let me go. This isn't any of your business, Cade. Stay out of this."

Despite her protests, she didn't once try to yank her arm away. She was wearing another weather-appropriate sweater, material much thicker than the thin dress Blondie/Cassie/Addie had been wearing, but my hand felt the heat of her skin. Heat so intense my palm burned, and I wondered if I'd ever be able to let it go or if I'd be fused to her forever.

Eventually, one of the doors I tried was unlocked. I opened it, glancing at the sign that said Business Center before stepping in and pulling her with me, then turning us so that my back was blocking the door.

"What is your problem?" Now she jerked her arm and stumbled, apparently surprised when I let her go right away.

I guess that answered that question.

I shoved my still burning hand into my pocket. "I don't have a problem. You, it seems, do."

"It's not a problem that needs you."

"It's not? I thought I came to New York specifically so you could ask me to help with your problem."

"I don't need help with money."

"Is this why you want him gone? Because he cut you off?" That son of a bitch, if he did. I was beginning to want him dead after all.

"It's not that simple." Her mouth quivered, and I recognized it as a gesture she made when she was on the edge of breaking down.

God, if she cried...

I might kill *her* if she pulled that on me. I couldn't deal with tears from anyone, least of all her. Especially when I couldn't know if they were real or a manipulative tactic.

I leaned my back against the door, getting comfortable. "Tell me the complicated version then."

She folded her arms across her chest and shot me a death glare. After a long, silent minute, she spoke. "You can't keep this room blocked off forever."

I surveyed our surroundings. For a nice hotel, it was a pathetic business center. Just a desk with two computers and a printer on it. Most likely, the type of clientele that stayed here had the hotel concierge handle any of their needs for them.

In other words, we weren't going to be bothered anytime soon. "Let's just see if I can't. I'm waiting."

"You'll be waiting a long time then because I don't owe you any explanation."

I could have begged to disagree.

But she was right about one thing—I couldn't keep her in

this room forever. Because every second that passed with her two feet away—her cherry-blossom scent tickling my nose, her lips trembling and tempting, her eyes big and penetrating—was a torturous second. Her features and gestures were too achingly familiar. The longer I stood in here with her, the closer I was to giving in.

Giving in to what, I didn't know. Giving in to everything.

I needed another tactic before I lost my grip. "You told the clerk you need the room until Friday. Is that when you're leaving New York?"

She sighed. "My flight home is Friday night."

I didn't let myself wonder where *home* was. "You can't change your flight?"

"Not without an outrageous change fee." Now that I wasn't asking about the particulars of how she got in her situation, she seemed more forthcoming.

"And you don't know anyone else in town?"

Her arms dropped to her sides, and she shook her head slowly, reluctantly, as though it cost her something to let me know that.

Probably because that meant she'd come just for me. She'd booked a whole week here, just for me.

She seemed to read my mind. "I didn't know how much time it would take to get you on my side."

"Seems you didn't count on me shutting you down on day one."

She shrugged, and I had a feeling the shrug meant she hadn't really accepted yet that I had shut her down. She sure as hell wasn't going to be closer to accepting it if I stepped in and helped her out.

Don't do it. Do not do it.

Just like that, I was back there again, to the past. *"He has money in his safe at the cabin. Gobs of it. I'll give you the combo. Take all of it, Cade. Every penny."*

It hadn't been hers to offer, but if she'd had money of her own, she would have drained her piggy bank for me. Whether or not she'd ever planned to leave with me, I knew she wouldn't have let me go empty-handed.

Without that stolen cash from her father, I would have had to do a lot uglier things than I had to survive.

With a groan, I wiped my palm over my beard. The money might have saved me, but I didn't owe her shit. Still, I couldn't leave a woman stranded in New York City. Not even her. "I'll pay your hotel bill. Let me get to a cash machine, and I can give you some extra for anything else you need."

And I could take the next flight out to Tokyo and not think about her ever again.

Her eyes flashed with the spitfire temper I remembered from her. "No way. I'm not a charity case."

I laughed. "You'll ask me to commit murder, but you can't take my money?"

"I was hoping you'd be invested in that for yourself." Her arms were folded across her chest again, in just the right way so it propped up her breasts, and fuck, I did not need to be thinking about her tits right now.

I focused my eyes on hers, refusing to let them drift lower. "Well, I'm not, and if the whole reason you want your father dead is because you need money, then you should just cut out the murder part and take mine." I'd give her more than what I'd offered. I'd write her a blank check.

I seriously hated myself for it, but it was true.

"I don't need your money." She stuck out her chin. Insistent. "I do fine."

"'Fine,' but you're getting kicked out of your hotel room—"

"Fine doesn't mean I can spare the money for an impromptu trip to NYC and a fancy hotel room. Regular people don't have gobs of cash lying around."

The comment about regular people hit me in the gut. Because I'd always been the regular one, and she'd never been anything close to "regular."

But I understood what she was saying. She wasn't desperate. She could take care of herself. She just couldn't take care of *this*, and to make matters worse, the reason she'd splurged on *this* was because she'd put all of her hope in me saying I'd help her out, and I refused.

"Then let me pay for the room," I said, softer. I didn't have any reason to feel guilty, and I didn't, but I could help her out. It wasn't a rescue. It was being a good human.

"You're not paying for my room."

"Let me—"

"I said you're not paying for my room."

"Then you can stay in my room." It was out of my mouth before I had time to think it through. I imagined I looked as shocked as she did about it.

She had the decency to realize it was something I never should have said. "I can't stay with you, Cade."

She was right. She couldn't. Worst idea on the planet. "It's a suite. There's plenty of space."

"I...can't..."

"I'm either paying for your room or you're staying in mine. Choose, Jol—." I caught myself. "Choose."

"You're not paying for my room." Stubborn, defiant. Like she'd always been.

Well, she'd made her choice.

And I was as stubborn and defiant as she was.

I whirled around, opened the door, and trekked down the hallway back toward the front desk.

"Cade? What are you doing now? Whatever it is, no." She followed after me, skipping now and then to keep up.

Ignoring her, I pulled my wallet out of my back pocket, went up to the desk clerk, and laid my ID and a hundred in front of him. "Add her to my room. She'll need her own key. Then have a bellhop help her move her stuff over."

It was outrageous and showy to give a hundred dollar tip, but I had a point to prove. I had money. Helping her out like this was nothing. She could have just let me pay for her room.

She stood next to me, silent, vibrating again, this time with rage, but also relief. I could feel it, and if I didn't know her better—and it could be argued that I didn't know her at all—I might have thought I'd been conned.

"Thank you," she said when it was all settled, and the clerk had called a bellhop and given her a key. I could tell it was hard for her to say it, but it didn't make me any less pissed.

I picked up my duffel bag. "You're sleeping on the couch."

"Of course."

"I'm sure you can find your way to the room on your own." I turned toward the front doors, needing the boxing club more now than ever.

Before I'd taken a step, she put a hand out on my bicep to stop me. "I want to be honest with you. It's like you said—I'm still here because I'm hoping you'll change your mind. I want you to know I'm going to take advantage of this situation."

I should have been scared. Instead, I took it as a challenge. "Go ahead and try."

I could take advantage of the situation too, I told myself as I stormed out into the cold December day. I could learn her secrets. I could leave no reason to still be curious. I could get my closure.

Or I could end up right where I'd always been—on my knees in love with a woman who would never love me back.

TEN

"Oh, it's you." Sabrina appeared just as surprised to see me when she opened Donovan's door as I was to see her. "I thought you were our lunch."

She stepped back so I could walk in past her. "Domesticating together already?" I'd known Donovan long enough to know he'd never had women in his apartment. He didn't even let them in for a romp before kicking them out. He didn't let them in period.

Based on Sabrina's outfit, which consisted of men's boxer shorts and an oversized T-shirt, it was obvious she'd stayed the night. And she was still here in the afternoon.

When the man said "girlfriend," he went all the way.

Sabrina apparently wasn't yet comfortable with their relationship status. "Uh...I mean, um. We had some work to go over..." She couldn't look at me, her cheeks bright pink.

I chuckled. "It's okay. Don't worry about it. No explanation needed. Is he here?"

"In his office." She nodded toward the stairs, but I was already headed in that direction. I knew the layout of the place, having stayed there several times over the course of our relationship. I was probably more familiar with the place than she was.

I bounded up the stairs two at a time, then knocked once on the closed door. I didn't wait for a reply before I opened it.

Donovan glanced up from his computer without moving his head. "I thought it was too fast for the food to be here. You're here sooner than I expected as well."

I looked at my watch. I'd spent a couple of hours at the boxing club, then hit the sauna before heading over to his building. Still, it was early in the day, only a little past one. "You said afternoon. It's after noon."

"Not complaining." He closed out of whatever he was working on and swung his chair to face me. "I just figured you'd be battling a mighty hangover today."

"Fuck you. I've even been to the gym already." I'd rented a locker at the club so I didn't have the duffel to prove it.

"Good for you. Have a cigar." He picked up the ornate box from the corner of his desk and handed it toward me.

I shook my head. "You look cozy. Playing house with her, are you?"

He set the cigar box down and pulled one out for himself before giving me a look that said I'm-not-discussing-my-girl-friend-with-you.

"And yet you want me to discuss Jolie with you."

He bit off the end of his cigar, then pointed it at me. "The difference is you don't want to hear my shit with Sabrina. I do want to hear your shit with Jolie. So you gonna lay it on me or what?"

I couldn't protest because it was true. I didn't want to hear about his happy love life. I was too bitter and jealous. Fuck him for being lucky enough to have everything work out. Must be fucking nice.

My expression must have told him exactly what I was thinking.

"Oh, come on," he said, standing up. He walked around the desk to me and stuck the cigar in my face. "Sit down. Smoke with me. You want to tell me, and I want to hear. Don't make me have to work to get it out of you."

I held my scowl for another few seconds before taking the offering and putting it in my mouth. Donovan was there instantly with a light. I puffed, getting the cherry nice and red while he returned to his chair and lit one for himself. "I hate these, you know."

"But you enjoy burning up my cash. These are Gurkhas. Seven-fifty a stick. Hate it less now?"

He knew me so well. I really did get a kick out of wasting his money. I cracked a small smile as I sat down in his leather armchair. "Marginally."

"That's what I thought."

The room filled with the scent of cognac and tobacco as we puffed silently. I knew where to start, and as he'd guessed, I was anxious to tell him, but now that I was here sitting down with him, it felt a little less urgent. Like maybe I'd made it all up in my mind. Not her visit, because that had definitely happened, but the atrocity of her request. Was I making it a bigger deal than it was? I'd told her no, I meant no, was there really anything to say about it?

I supposed that was what I was here to figure out.

"She wants my help with something," I said eventually,

glad that Donovan hadn't pushed me to say it before I was ready.

"Figured as much. She disappeared for all these years. Couldn't imagine she'd pop up again unless she was desperate. Are you going to help her?"

"You're not even going to ask what it is?" I was sure he would have wanted to know that first thing. Here he was jumping past the most important part.

"The favor is less interesting than your response."

"But how can you decide if my response is justified if you don't know what the favor is?"

He tapped his finger on his cigar, then leaned forward. "You really are going to make me work for this." There was the Donovan I knew.

I inhaled deeply on my cigar, taking in more tobacco than I needed, but damn the buzz felt good. "She wants me to kill her father."

He didn't bat an eye. "Does he deserve it?"

"Uh. Does anyone?"

"Yes. There are most definitely people who deserve it, and you know that as well as I do. You've worked with a fair number of them."

Sure, I'd worked with some despicable men in my life, but I hadn't ever sat around contemplating a death wish list. "I've never thought it was my responsibility to make it happen."

"It's not. Unless you decide it is. Have you decided it is this time?"

"I can't believe you're calmly sitting there, casually asking me if I'm going to murder my ex-girlfriend's prick of a father."

"If that was the entire extent of the relationship you had

with Stark, I'd maybe be more worked up about it." He considered his words. "Nah. Probably not."

I wasn't sure what I'd been expecting. Calm, collected, cool-as-a-cucumber Donovan Kincaid didn't get in a fuss about much of anything. Why had I thought this would be any different? "She should have asked you to help her out."

"She still could. Want me to find someone?"

I couldn't decide if he was messing with me or if he was sincere. Or if he actually knew someone who did that kind of job.

Whatever the answer, my response was the same. "You helping her is the same as me helping her, and I'm not fucking helping her."

"Because the favor itself turns you off or you don't want to help her at all?"

"Both." It wasn't true. I wanted it to be, but I'd offered her money and a place to stay within twenty-four hours of our initial meeting. "The first one. Frankly, you should be turned off by it too."

He ignored my attack on his morals. "Then if she'd asked something else, something less..."

"Illegal," I filled in for him.

He gave me a knowing glare. He knew legality had never been a problem for me. "Something less *life ending*, you would have helped her out."

I didn't know how to answer that. Honestly, I was appalled she had the gall to ask for anything from me at all, and if her favor had been anything else—if she'd asked for me to give her a recommendation or sign a get well card, anything at all—I would have probably turned her down. Because she deserved to be the disappointed one this time. Because how dare she?

The only reason I'd helped her out today was because it hadn't been as satisfying to turn her down yesterday as I'd wanted it to be.

"I don't know, Donovan. I don't know what I would have said if her request had been something reasonable. I think I would have turned her down no matter what."

"But you'd still be thinking about it today."

I didn't have to respond. I was here, wasn't I?

ELEVEN

"So I'll ask again—does he deserve it?"

It was a moot point as far as I was concerned, since there was no way I was helping, but as long as Donovan wanted to go down this road, well. It could be interesting to see where it led. "Stark was...not nice."

"So I've gathered from what you've said in the past."

"Abusive for sure. Physically. The kind of abusive that Child Protective Services would want to put behind bars."

"But you could never prove it."

"No."

"And he wasn't like that with other students?" He was familiar with the charges I'd tried to bring against my former headmaster, though I'd never gone into detail. It seemed he'd done some research of his own, or had at least figured out enough of the parts I'd left out to know what to ask.

"Nope. I was special." The wrong kind of special.

"Yeah, well, you know why that is."

I was quiet for a second, remembering all the reasons that man had hated me from day one. "Yeah. I suppose I do."

"Not your fault. You dealt with the cards you were handed." He rolled his cigar between his lips. "But you're saying he wasn't really a danger to anyone after you were gone?"

My instinct was no. Though I couldn't have said what he'd done after I'd left.

There was also a chance I'd been a buffer for his brutal nature. And with me gone, he could very well have gotten his sadistic kicks elsewhere, including on Jolie.

My mind started to wander to someone else who might have been his victim, someone other than Jolie, but I shut that line of thinking down right away, unwilling to follow it. It was bad enough thinking he might have used his daughter for his punching bag with me gone. I didn't have room to worry about anyone else.

But Langdon Stark's danger didn't just lie in his hands. "On paper, no. He was a model headmaster who ran a model school. He produced the best students who got into the best colleges. The parents who sent their kids there didn't care about methods. They wanted results."

"So they didn't care if the guy in charge smacked them around a bit?"

"No, not that. I really don't think he laid a hand on anyone else. At least, I couldn't find anyone who would admit it when I was looking for corroboration when I filed charges. But he was..." I paused, trying to think how to describe it. The man was a gaslighter and a master manipulator. Looking back, it was just as hard to identify what was so horrible about him as when I'd been in the middle of it.

"This one time, for instance," I said, deciding it was better to give him an example. "I was still new to the place, but a couple of the guys were feeling me out. Seeing if I was worthy of their time or friendship. This kid, Birch—I don't remember his first name. He was a total asswipe. So of course he was popular. He liked to write these horrid stories about the people he didn't like. He thought they were funny, and of course anyone he shared them with would laugh like they were because he was a guy with that kind of power, but they were really just mean. Stories about how slutty the girl in math class was or how the kid with the glasses had a limp dick.

"So this day, he wrote a particularly nasty thing about the fat kid. Presley." I'd never forget him—wide eyes hidden behind round glasses that only made his face look heavier. Smart, but shy. Decent. Nice. "I mean, this story went on and on about Presley's size, how he'd never get laid, and if he even tried he'd end up rolling over on the girl and killing her with his weight."

"Sounds like we need to take a hit out on this Birch guy," Donovan said. As though taking a hit out on someone was everyday for him.

"Eh. Birch was a prick, but he was harmless for the most part. Most of his victims never knew they were being made fun of. Except this time, the story had been passed to me, and I was reading it behind my history book, pretending to laugh as I did so he'd think I was cool. Or maybe I really did think it was funny. It's hard to have that perspective in the aftermath. Anyway, Stark was subbing for the professor that day, and he caught me."

"Uh-oh."

It had been ridiculously stupid for me to have been acting up in front of him. I should have been on my best behavior the minute he'd walked in the room. Even new, I'd figured that much out in my encounters with him.

But I'd been seventeen and a rebel, and I'd wanted to fit in, and that need outweighed any sense of survival. "And instead of just sending me to detention or dealing with me privately later on, he turned the whole thing into a spectacle. Brought me up to the front of the class. Made me read the whole thing out loud."

"Okay...and?" Donovan seemed to need help seeing the point.

"And it was awful. Not for me, necessarily—though yes for me, too, because like hell was I saying who really wrote it, and so of course most everyone thought it was me. But the worst part was that Presley was in the class, and he had to hear it. I could understand the nature of the punishment, truly I could. But as soon as Stark heard what sort of story it was, he should have stopped me and dealt with me later. That's what a decent educator would have done.

"Not Stark. He prodded me on. He made me read every cruel word, made Presley listen as I made fun of his size in every wicked way possible. Made me keep going, even after Presley had started to openly cry. I tried to keep my eyes on the paper so I wouldn't see his face, but I couldn't miss the sound of his sobbing. And when I glanced at Stark, praying he'd let me stop, he had the most gleeful look in his eyes. Orgasmic. Like he was in heaven."

"Sounds like a true sadist." Donovan tapped the growing ash off the end of his cigar into an ashtray.

"Mm," I murmured in agreement. Then I dropped my own cigar in the tray, feeling too sick from the memory to smoke anymore. "I could recount a dozen stories like that. He didn't lay a hand on his students, but he was psychologically abusive."

"Psychological abuse is quite often worse than physical."

"But harder to identify." I waited a beat, then added, "Harder to justify murdering over."

Donovan raised a shoulder as though not quite sure he agreed. "I imagine his treatment of his students isn't the reason Jolie wants him gone."

It was my turn to shrug. "She wouldn't say why."

"She wouldn't?" Finally, Donovan seemed surprised.

"Wouldn't tell me why now or why me."

"Hard to ask someone for such a heavy favor without having a reason. She offer to pay you?"

"No, no. No." I paused, not sure I wanted to say more. But it was Donovan, and I always told him everything. "I think she's broke, actually. Might be why she came to me. Because she thought I might do it for her without compensation. I was probably one of a whole list of ex-boyfriends she approached to do the deed."

He shook his head. "I doubt that. Still seems hard to expect you to be motivated without more information."

"Right."

"Has to be something pretty important though. Something specific. To bring her out of hiding."

I leaned back in the chair, considering. This was what I liked about my partnership with Donovan—he thought differently than I did. He looked at the whole picture while I was focused on the minutia. He followed trails of thinking that I would never see and ended up with an understanding of situations that was often out of my scope of comprehension.

Regardless...

"It doesn't matter what her reason is. I'm not helping her, and I'm not covering for her if someone comes asking me questions later on."

"Then that's it. Your decision's made." He didn't sound like he was trying to dispute me. More like he was trying to confirm.

"Yep."

"Great. You're done with this and her; you can move on."

"Yeah. Exactly how I was looking at it." Well. Except. "Actually, not quite done with *her* yet..."

He raised a quizzical eyebrow, and with his black turtleneck and slacks, he looked more like a behind-the-scenes mastermind than usual.

For some reason, that made it harder to want to admit my fuckup. But he'd find out one way or another. Donovan had a way like that. "Like I said, it seems she's got a money problem. Couldn't afford to keep her hotel through until she leaves. Refused to take money from me for it. So I told her she could stay with me." I said the last part fast. Like ripping off a Band-Aid.

Now both of his eyebrows rose. "Seems you weren't opposed to helping her after all."

"It's barely helping her," I protested. "I wanted her off my conscience. That's all." It had nothing to do with the way my chest felt tight when I was near her or the way her gaze pierced into my soul.

"Off your conscience, into your bed. Sounds right."

I gave him a stern stare. "I'm not going to fuck her."

"Want to bet on that?"

Last time I'd made a bet with Donovan, I'd ended up with *Gangster* tattooed across my back. I vowed never to make that mistake again.

But it was impossible not to want to show him up. He always acted so superior. Like he knew everything and everyone better than they knew themselves. And maybe if I had a bet with him, I wouldn't be tempted to even consider letting something sexual happen with Jolie.

Not that I was considering sex as it was. I definitely wasn't.

"Sure thing. I win, and you get the tattoo of my choice this time." I already had it planned out—a heart with flowers and the word *Mom*.

"When I win, that will be two tattoos you don't want on your skin. You ready for that?"

"Not going to lose, and I'm definitely ready to see you in ink."

"You're on." He was too far away to shake on it, but a nod sealed the deal. He grinned like I was a fool. "This day just took an eventful turn. Glad to have you back in town. How long are you here?"

I hadn't booked a return flight yet. Every instinct said I should get on a plane sooner rather than later. If I got something out tonight, I could stop by the hotel, gather my things, and not have to see Jolie ever again. I'd picked up the phone to make a reservation at least three times since I'd first had the thought. Twice I'd started a text to have my assistant do it.

Then I'd think about what was waiting for me at home— enough work to keep me busy. Designer sheets that only ever smelled like me. A list of revolving hookups who didn't mind meeting in hotel rooms.

Arguably the perfect life.

I had no logical reason to stay, and a million good reasons to run, but I was stuck again in that tar pit that surrounded Jolie.

Desperately wanting to get out but unable to make myself move.

"I guess I'm leaving Saturday," I said. She'd be gone then. I'd be able to leave.

"Jolie must be flying out Friday." His grin widened. "Got any blank skin on your torso? I want to pick the best spot for your new art."

"Fuck you."

"You mean fuck her."

I refused to reply. We sat quietly again, and I mulled over everything we'd talked about, trying to decide if I'd gained any perspective from our conversation. Usually talking with Donovan helped shift my view, but everything looked exactly the way it had when I'd walked in. I was just as adamant that I wasn't going to kill Stark as when I'd arrived. I was just as pissed that she'd asked me. I was just as determined to hate her forever.

Fucking her hadn't crossed my mind before Donovan put the idea in my head, but I was just as resolute about that as well.

"Do you have to kill him literally?" Donovan asked, interrupting my what-a-waste-of-time thought spiral.

He was always trying to figure out the way that most of the people involved came out a winner, usually with him the biggest winner of them all. It was abnormally altruistic for him to care when he wasn't eligible for a prize.

His question was intriguing, though. "What do you mean?"

Before he could answer, the buzzer rang. "Food must be here," he said but let Sabrina answer it. He put his cigar out. "You can stay. We ordered extra yakisoba in case you came by."

It was tempting. It had been the better part of the year

since I'd had a meal with my friend, and nothing sounded more relaxing than kicking back with a beer and shooting the shit with him over Japanese.

But he was with Sabrina now. And I had Jolie to deal with. Or rather, Jolie to avoid. With our bet made, it was unlikely Donovan would be supportive in that endeavor.

"Next time," I said, standing up. "You have house to play. Should we wager how long before there's a ring on her finger?" I held out my hand to shake goodbye if he didn't take me up on the bet.

"Not a chance," he said, taking my hand. "Unlike you, I know when the odds are against me."

He didn't fucking know anything. Not a single goddamned thing.

But I was definitely going to stay away from my suite for the rest of the day, just to be sure.

TWELVE

I spent the rest of the afternoon back at Reach, using Weston's office so I didn't have to be reminded of the last time I was in Donovan's. After that, I joined Nate at the gentleman's club the guys liked to frequent, which wasn't the worst of distractions, despite the fact that he had a new lady he couldn't shut up about.

At least his lady wasn't the lady I was trying to not think about, and so I endured the torture until well after midnight when I finally gave up the battle and headed back to my hotel.

Headed back to *her*.

Outside my room, I took a beat to prepare myself, then opened the door to the best case scenario—a dark living area, suggesting my guest was already asleep. Just as I'd hoped.

I avoided looking at the direction of the sofa as I headed toward my room. A lamp had been left on, and the low murmur of voices told me I'd left the TV on as well. I didn't have a chance to realize I hadn't turned on the television before I'd made it to the doorway and saw who apparently did: Jolie. Asleep. On my bed. Wearing nothing but a T-shirt and panties.

Emotions crashed through me like lightning, striking and disappearing so fast, I barely had time to acknowledge them. Once upon a time, this was supposed to have been our life. Her, sleeping in my bed like it was no big deal. Me, eager not to disturb her as I gazed down at her soft features.

But we hadn't gotten the happily ever after.

And this was not our life.

"What the fuck, Julianna? I said sleep on the couch." My voice boomed loud enough to wake her with a start.

She blinked, confused for a moment. Then she saw me and stretched. "Hey! You're here." There was a note of relief in her tone. As though she were glad I'd shown up. As though she'd been afraid I wouldn't.

It was fucked up how the instinct to run to her was still so easily triggered in my body.

I was as mad at that response as I was her. "Yeah. Because it's my room. If you wanted to treat it like your own, you could have stayed in yours, like I originally offered."

"No. This is good. This is great. I mean the couch is great." She jumped off the bed and gathered herself before explaining. "The TV out there isn't working. I have a hard time sleeping when I'm alone unless it's on, so I figured I'd just hang out here until you got here. I didn't mean to fall asleep. I'm sorry."

It was after one in the morning. Of course she was falling asleep.

There was no accusation in her tone, though, which almost pissed me off even more.

But also, I didn't trust her.

"The TV doesn't work?" I flicked on the light switch,

noting that the couch hadn't even been made into a bed yet, then stomped over to the living area television set, ready to call bullshit. While I wasn't sure that she was particularly manipulative, she *had* said that she'd try to take advantage of this situation, and seduction had always been her weapon of choice. The broken TV seemed like an awfully convenient setup.

But when I tried the power button, sure enough, it didn't turn on. I found the cord behind the set and followed it to the wall.

"It's plugged in," she said from behind me.

Yeah, but had she tried it in another outlet? I unplugged it and scanned the wall for another place to try it.

"I checked the outlet too. My phone cord works in it, so it's not that."

"You should have—"

She cut me off, reading my thoughts. "I called the front desk. They came up and fiddled with it and said they'd have a new one delivered tomorrow. They offered to give us a different room, but I didn't want to make that decision for you."

So not a scam then.

I looked around for something else to be mad at and found it easily. That T-shirt she was wearing? It was mine. "It's hard to not think you're up to something when you're lounging around on *my* bed, wearing *my* clothes."

"You're so very perceptive. I was very much up to something. Want to know what it was?" She'd sauntered toward me while she spoke, and now she was an inch away, leaning in like she was about to share her greatest secret.

I could barely breathe. "What?"

"Sleeping." She flashed a huge smile, popping the tension like it was a balloon and she was a pin. "I'm pretty transparent,

Cade. I've already laid out what I'm up to, and save for a couple of personal secrets, I'm not really hiding anything."

She was definitely not hiding a lot dressed like that. Her legs were long and toned and curved in just the right places. It was hard to ignore how beautiful she was. How beautiful she'd always been.

I wasn't distracted enough by her looks, though, to miss the implication of her words. She was basically inviting me to ask her anything. Anything at all. I could have all the answers I'd been seeking. I could ask about all the unknown details of her life that had kept me awake for countless nights over the years. The bits of Jolie trivia that had driven me crazy with burning curiosity.

Or maybe that was her game. Lull me into a false sense of trust. Then attack.

I refused to let my guard down. "Okay, then, so you won't mind telling me why you're wearing my shirt."

She took a step back and leaned against the arm of the couch. Comfortably, not seductively. "It's not as exciting as the reason you're alluding to. I usually sleep in just..." She gestured to her panties. Cotton and plain, like the kind she'd worn as a teen. "All the clothes I brought with me are weather appropriate. Sweaters. Jeans. Nothing comfortable enough to sleep in."

"So you went through my stuff?"

That smile again. "I don't remember you being so suspicious and melodramatic."

"I don't remember you having a total lack of respect for privacy."

Her smile faded then because we were talking about my things, but we were talking about her secrets too. If she wanted me to respect her boundaries, she had to respect mine. "I opened one drawer and took the first shirt I found. That's it. I can give it back—" She grabbed the hem and lifted it high enough that I saw the bottom curve of her breasts.

My pants felt tighter.

"Stop." I looked away in case she didn't. "Keep it. Keep it for the week." I almost offered to let her take it with her when she left, but the plain black T had suddenly become one of my favorites.

"Thanks." Her smile was back, more contained than before, but genuine. "And for the room. I really do appreciate it."

I was still pissed. Anger was my security blanket, and if I let it go...

Well, I didn't want to think what I'd be left with then. So I didn't accept her apology or her gratitude. I just stood there feeling gruff and raw and turned inside out and let her make of it what she would.

"I'll, um, just..." She stood and nodded toward the couch behind her.

It was my cue to leave. To go hole up in my bedroom, with the dresser pushed against the door if necessary.

But that luxury room, with its king-size bed and thousand-thread-count sheets, suddenly seemed lonely. And just like she'd needed the TV on for companionship, I wanted to linger in her presence. "Here, I'll help you set it up."

I crossed to the opposite end of the couch and reached for a cushion. She hesitated only a beat before joining me, tossing cushions to the floor, then hefting the metal frame out of the enclosure. The mattress inside was bare, but I found a bag of bedding in the coat closet that included a bed sheet. I unfolded it and handed her an end.

Then together we spread it across the mattress, tucking the

ends around the corners so it would stay. I'd never made up a bed with someone before. This was the spot where she'd sleep. Where she'd spend hours at her most vulnerable. It was intimate in a way I hadn't expected. More intimate than sex even. I'd fucked a lot of women. Jolie hadn't even been my first. But for this, she was the only one.

I peeked over at her as we tucked the top sheet in. Her gaze brushed over mine in periphery, then caught it full on. My breath felt lodged in my chest, and I cleared my throat, as though that would help.

It didn't. But the noise strengthened her attention, and now I felt obliged to do something with it. "You're here a week," I said, not sure where I was going with the remark.

"Yeah."

"Because you thought that would be enough time...?"

"Enough time to convince you to help me?" She pulled a pillow to her so she could put on a pillowcase. "I hoped it was enough time."

I tried to consider her position and what she knew of me. What she knew of the boy I'd once been. That kid, would he have helped her? How long would it have taken for him to be convinced?

Not even a full minute.

"I could already have been on my way out of the city by now. How could you be sure I would even be here for a full week?"

"It's a long flight. The odds seemed to be in favor that you wouldn't just turn around and go back."

"But we had no arrangements to see each other again. As far as you knew, you had that one meeting. That's all I'd given you."

She smiled guiltily. "Why do you think I made sure I was staying in your hotel?"

A hotel with a near thousand-dollar-a-night price tag. She probably would have had enough to charge the whole week if she'd booked something on Priceline.

It had been an expensive gamble on her part. "That's a lot of guesswork. A lot of things had to fall into place to be sure you saw me again."

"Hard to knock my plan when I'm staying in your room."

I caught myself before I laughed out loud. Admittedly, she was cute—had always been cute. A little full of herself. A lot full of determination. I'd already spent enough time with her to see that hadn't changed. As much as I refused to acknowledge it, there was a lot of that girl I'd known still in this woman, and that realization made me nostalgic.

Made me start thinking things I shouldn't.

I was grateful when Donovan's words from earlier butted into my thoughts. *Do you have to kill him literally?*

"Why do you need him to be dead? Are you that set on revenge?" I was an idiot. Practically asking her to change my mind.

"Not just revenge."

"Then what? Money?"

She shook her head as she unfolded the comforter. "I need him out of my life. Can you take the end?"

I took the other side of the blanket and spread it over the bed, but I ignored her attempt to change the conversation. "Do you still live near him? Do you need help moving away?"

Headmaster Stark was a prominent figure in his community. She was a full-grown woman, but if they lived in the same town, there was no way she could really escape him. Was that all it was? She had enough money to live, but maybe not enough money to reestablish herself away from him?

"No, I've lived in Boston for about ten years."

Boston.

One word, but it was a puzzle piece I'd been searching for for so long that I couldn't help but hold on to it once she'd given it. *Boston.* All this time, she'd been in Boston.

Boston wasn't that far from Connecticut, though. "Is he bothering you? Showing up on your doorstep?"

"It's not quite that simple—"

"You keep saying that. I have resources that can handle complicated."

The blanket in place, she stood up straight. "I need him out of my life *for good.*"

There was desperation in her voice that I recognized because it was exactly the desperation I'd felt back then, when I didn't see any escape from her father's abuse. She'd suffered at his hand too, but I'd never seen the despair in her that I saw now.

What hold did he still have over her?

Trying to convince myself I didn't care was futile. At the very least, I was curious. "What did he—"

She cut me off. "I'm not going to say any more than that, Cade. Please don't ask."

Transparent, my ass.

Fuck her.

"Looks like you're good here. I'll leave you to it."

I brushed off her good night and walked around the bed to head to my room without a word. I did look back, though. Not to check out her ass, but since she was reaching across the bed to straighten the edge of the comforter, that's exactly what I saw.

And then I froze, my eyes pinned on the art inked at her hip, visible as the shirt rose with her stretch.

Before I knew what I was doing, I was at her side, tugging down the side of her panties far enough to see the whole thing.

"Hey!" She was startled but not incensed. In fact, once she realized what I was looking at, she lifted the shirt so I could see the full-color design better—a bird cage, the bars torn open in one spot, one bird outside the cage in flight, another still sitting inside.

I knelt down at her side, my breath caught in my chest, my heart pounding in my ears. Wordlessly, I swept my finger across her skin. Goosebumps broke out underneath my touch. Strange, since my finger felt like it was burning as it moved over the broken cage. Over the bird in the sky. Over the bird behind the bars. I lingered here the longest, tracing the creature's wings.

Why hasn't she flown away?

I would have traded places with her. If one of us had had to stay, I would have done that. If that had been an option. If that had been the price for her freedom.

Her belly rose with an intake of air, and I realized she'd been holding her breath. Realized I was touching her. Realized I was on the brink of falling apart.

I stood up quickly, careful not to meet her eyes. "Hey, how about you go ahead and take the bedroom? So you can keep the TV on," I added, so she wouldn't think the offer was for any reason other than practicality.

She tugged her shirt—my shirt—down, and folded her arms

across her chest, as if by covering up, I could unsee what I'd seen. "I'm not doing that."

"You said you can't sleep."

"I should be better knowing you're in the next room. If not, I'll put YouTube on my phone."

She wouldn't look at me either. God, she was so frustrating. "Just take the room, Jo—" I caught myself. "Julianna."

Now her eyes hit mine, and I could practically hear her thoughts. *"It's Jolie now."* But she managed to refrain from saying it.

And I managed to refrain from saying the other thing pressing on my tongue, that I could take the room with her. That I could make her feel less alone. That I could still help her fly.

"Just for tonight," I insisted. Needing her in that other room as soon as fucking possible. "Okay?"

If she had fought with me right then, I didn't know what I would have done, but I had a feeling it would have been something impossible to come back from.

Fortunately, she didn't fight. I sat on the couch bed and busied myself with taking off my shoes, not looking up again until after I'd heard the click of the door shut behind her.

THIRTEEN

I slept fitfully, and not because the bed was uncomfortable, though it really was too small for my height. It was her keeping me up. She was quiet as a mouse, the only sound coming from the bedroom the low drone of the television. But I *felt* her. And every time I started to drift off, I jerked awake, as though my brain had determined I couldn't waste a single second of being in her presence with sleep.

I must have slept eventually because sometime around seven in the morning I woke up. There was no foggy daze where I temporarily forgot she was in the next room. As soon as my eyes opened, my ears were straining, listening for any of her sounds, imagining I could hear the soft rhythm of her breathing.

Cursing at myself, I rolled out of bed and tugged on last night's clothes so I wouldn't have to deal with her. Thankfully, the bathroom wasn't an en suite, and I was able to slip in, relieve myself, and freshen up without disturbing her.

I was out the door before she made a single peep.

The boxing club was busier at this time of the day. Being Monday didn't help; the place filled with Midtowners getting a workout in before heading to the office. Somehow, I managed to get a bag to myself, and I set out to keep my thoughts from overtaking me with pure aggression.

But even after an hour of beating the shit out of my imaginary opponent, I had enough energy to scare myself. Twice, I was invited into the ring for a real fight. Twice, I declined, afraid I'd kill someone.

Kill the *wrong* someone.

Fuck, I couldn't escape it, couldn't escape *her* or her damn favor. Couldn't punch away the thoughts and the memories and the desires. The desire to save her. The desire to fix her. The desire to have her as mine again.

I was sore and exhausted by the time I finally gave up and changed out of my gym clothes. After the long workout, the cold outside felt good, and I loitered outside the club, letting the nine-to-fivers hurry past while I soaked in the chill.

Not too much later, someone else paused as he stepped out of the club, long enough to pull a smoke out of his pocket and get it lit.

"Can I bum one?" I hadn't even made the conscious decision to ask before the words were out.

The guy looked me over, probably deciding if I meant to mug him or if I really just wanted a cigarette. Then he pulled the pack out and handed me one followed by his lighter.

"Thanks, man." I inhaled just enough to light the end before handing the lighter back. When he was on his way and I was alone again, I took a long drag and inhaled deeply.

Instantly, I was back there. Back to the night she'd kissed

my stripes. She'd slipped out later to meet me at our spot. As she crouched down next to me, I handed her the cigarette I'd been smoking, then lit another for myself.

She hadn't had to say anything for me to know he'd punished her too. For what, it didn't matter. For helping me. For being caught with me. For something else entirely.

"Was it...terrible?" I cringed because of course it was terrible. It was always terrible.

She stared out into the distance and didn't answer, which wasn't unusual. She didn't like to talk about the punishments. Fortunately, she didn't get them very often. Not as often as I did anyway. Headmaster Stark must have really been on a tear today.

I reached a hand out to settle on her arm. "Do I need to be putting antibiotic on your back?"

She took a drag off her cigarette, then blew it out before answering. "He doesn't like to leave marks on me."

I wanted to hold her, but she didn't like to be held when she was in this mood. She seemed to think it was a suffering she had to handle on her own, and no matter how many times I tried to tell her differently, tried to tell her we were in this together and she didn't have to take it on alone, I'd yet to convince her.

It tore me up inside that I couldn't bear it for her. It was agony worse than any punishment her father could give.

"We're going to fly away, Jol," I said, wanting to give her the hope she'd given me earlier. It sounded stupid when I said it to myself, but out loud to her, it was a promise.

She looked at me then, looked at my hand resting at my side next to hers. Then she linked her pinkie in mine, and I wondered if she knew that she'd saved me, just by being there, just by being *who she was, and I prayed with all my soul that I could do the same for her.*

Praying had obviously gotten me nowhere.

Or was it only now that those prayers were being answered?

I tossed my unfinished cigarette in the snow. My muscles were stiff from the cold, but I pushed them forward, trucking back to the hotel at top speed, urgency buzzing in my blood.

I pushed through the breakfast crowd in the lobby and hit the elevator button over and over, willing it to get there faster. Then once inside, I hit the floor button with as much vigor. Finally, I was bursting into the suite, then throwing open the bedroom door.

She was awake, but from the glazed way she looked at me, just barely.

"We won't kill him," I declared. "We'll destroy him."

Her brows furrowed as she tried to get context. Then she frowned. "But—"

"He'll be out of your life. For good." Whether we had to set him up or dig up a real scandal, we would bring Langdon Stark down.

I waited for her to argue. I could feel her on the brink of it, but if she was really as desperate as she said she was, then she'd take what she could get, and this was what I could give.

She must have realized that because all she said was, "Okay."

Then before she got all weepy or grateful, I set the record straight. "And I'm doing this for me. Not for you. Got it?"

"Okay."

"Okay," I repeated.

"Okay," she said again, the corners of her mouth lifting in a wary smile.

Okay. We were doing this. Okay.

Our eyes locked, and I could practically hear her echoing thoughts. *Finally, we're doing this. Okay.*

"Good. Get dressed. We leave in ten." I tore my eyes away, but not before noticing she'd lost the shirt sometime during the night and now only had the sheet wrapped around her.

No time for thinking about that. We had work to do. We had someplace to be.

And if we were going to do this, we were going to need Donovan.

FOURTEEN

Donovan's office wall was opaque, and his door was shut when we arrived. Which meant he was either with a client or he was in a mood.

I hoped it was the former.

"He alone in there, Simone?" I asked his secretary, the same one he'd had in Tokyo, so I knew her well.

"He is, but—"

There wasn't any but between partners. Still, it was probably best to go in by myself first in case he was rubbing one out under his desk. "Hang here a second," I told Jolie, then entered Donovan's office without knocking, ignoring Simone's protests.

He was at his desk—both hands visible and working, thank God—and only gave me a fleeting glance before turning back to his computer. "I don't have time for it."

I guffawed. "You don't even know what *it* is."

"Doesn't matter what it is, unless you're here to help me, and if you are I'm grateful for the offer, but seeing how you're dressed…" He gave a disapproving frown at my hoodie and jeans. "That doesn't appear to be the case, so go away."

His dismissive tone would have sent most of his subordinates scurrying away.

But I wasn't a subordinate. "You forget I've worked with you long enough to know you can handle a day's load in an hour and spend the rest of the day busying yourself with your other interests. Whatever side project you're obsessed with today, I have one that will top it."

It was the right bait, and he hesitated before shaking his head. "I have *actual* work to do. Weston's out on his honeymoon—"

Oh, whoa. Wait. "He's going on a real honeymoon for a fake wedding?"

"Would you quiet down?" He gestured toward the door, which I'd left slightly ajar. "And yes. It needs to look legit."

I kicked the door the rest of the way closed. "He's heard of internet, right? Surely he can still handle putting together marketing packages from a beach."

"Sabrina and I can handle it. But that means I need to be actually handling *it* and not *you*."

I bit my cheek so I wouldn't go off on his inference that I needed to be handled. "I'll pitch in with Weston's shit. Throw me at whatever. I'm yours to command."

Again, he looked tempted. I very rarely offered assistance. He had to be itching to take advantage of that.

But after a few seconds, he shook his head. "It'll be easier to just do it all myself."

I swallowed a growl and the urge to kick him in his arrogant nutsack, and forced myself to be on my best behavior. To be fair, I was showing up unannounced, expecting him to drop everything to dig up a scandal on a man who had tormented me almost two decades ago.

On the other hand, this was exactly Donovan's jam.

"Look, D, I wouldn't be here if I had another option. We need your help. The kind of help only you can give."

Finally, his hands moved off the keyboard. He swiveled in his chair, giving me his full attention. "You decided to do it?"

Got him.

I tried not to be too smug. "We're not going to kill him literally. We're going to kill him in the figurative sense."

"What a brilliant idea. Wonder where you got it?" Donovan didn't bother hiding his smugness at all. His eyes narrowed, his jaw working, and I knew he was already seven steps ahead of me, various ideas of vengeance playing out in his mind. "You're doing all the advertising performance reports."

Shit. Advertising reports were the fucking worst. "Fine."

"There's a significant stack."

He was gloating, but I refused to appear fazed. "Cool. Whatever." I opened the door, stuck my head out, and found Jolie sitting on the waiting area sofa. I gestured for her to join us and turned to Simone. "Make sure we aren't disturbed."

Simone was a professional who somehow managed to work with the likes of Donovan. Partner title or not, she wasn't about to take orders from me, and her single-raised eyebrow made sure I knew it.

Fortunately, her real boss intervened. "No disruptions unless it's Sabrina," he called out.

The guy was definitely whipped.

He defended himself without me saying anything. "She's been thrown into her boss's job. I'm not leaving her to that alone. It would be bad for the company."

"Right. It's about the company." I dropped it, though, as Jolie stepped in the room, passing by me. I hadn't given her a chance to shower, but she must have freshened up her perfume because that cherry-blossom scent drifted to my nose, mixed with the familiar scent of her, and while I'd never been a delicate kind of guy, my knees actually felt like they might buckle.

I pulled the door shut behind her, glad I had the knob to hold on to for support.

"Wasn't that wall see-through the other day?" she asked, first noticing the clouded glass before the domineering dickwad behind the desk.

I could have kissed her for that blow to Donovan's ego.

Not literally, of course.

Though now I was thinking about her lips when I had no business thinking about them.

"It transforms at the push of a button," Donovan explained as he came around his desk and walked over to us. "I prefer the opaque when I'm working. Less of a distraction." He threw a glare in my direction that I didn't have a chance to decipher before he stuck his hand out toward Jolie. "And since it doesn't look like this asshole is going to do it, I'm Donovan Kincaid."

Oh, right. Introductions. He already knew so much about her, it felt like they'd already met.

With a warm smile, she put her hand in his. "Jolie—" She stopped abruptly, as though she were about to say her last name and decided against it for some reason. "Jolie."

"Julianna Lucille Stark," I corrected. Because she might be trying to run away from who she'd been, but who she'd been was entirely the reason she was here right now.

Her smile went from warm to tight. "I go by Jolie now."

"Ah. So that's why we couldn't find you." He'd already

considered the possibility, of course, and had suggested it numerous times. *"Maybe she changed her name."*

"But wouldn't there be a record?" It hadn't occurred to me that she might have done it unofficially.

She turned her gaze toward me for the first time since meeting Donovan. "You looked for me?"

Her tone was genuinely surprised, which in turn, surprised me. I'd always assumed the reason I couldn't find her was because she hadn't wanted me to find her. But that presumed she'd expected me to look.

There was probably more to it to wonder about, but I was more concerned with what Donovan's slip gave away about *me*. Like the impression that I cared.

I did, obviously.

Or I had. I wasn't sure anymore which it was, but I was sure I didn't want her help figuring it out.

I shrugged, trying to blow it off. "Didn't look that hard. I don't talk to my mother anymore. Thought you could give me a bit of news from the home front." Plausible. Likely, even.

She held my gaze, though, looking at me in a new way, as if she saw more to me than she saw before. More than I wanted her to see.

Fucking Donovan.

I shot him daggers, which he returned with a smirk.

"Anyway, it's nice to meet you, Jolie. Let me take your coat." He helped her with it while I took off my own. "Ready to get started? I imagine we have a lot to get through."

He handed her coat to me to hang up, like I was the unnecessary component of this meeting, and ushered her to take a seat before returning to the other side of his desk.

Like I said before, fucking Donovan.

"I don't know what you've been told..." she said, twisting in her chair so she could see me at the closet.

See? I was still important here. "Assume Donovan knows everything. If I haven't already told him, he's figured it out on his own. He has a knack for..." I trailed off, weighing the desire to tell the truth with how much trouble it might get me in with him to say it.

"Knowing things?" he offered when I took too long.

"I was going to say getting involved in other people's shit without their invitation. But that works."

It earned me a glare. "It's that knack that's helping you right now, so I'd be careful with your attitude."

I shut the closet door harder than need be. I'd helped him out a time or two or seven. Perhaps I needed to remind him.

"Thank you for this," Jolie said sincerely. "If he hasn't said it yet."

"He hasn't. But I'm pretty sure I owe him one so there's no need." No reminder necessary, it seemed.

"Only owe me one?" I perched on the arm of the sofa.

He stared at me for a beat. "If we get into the game of who owes whom, Cade, we're going to waste a lot of valuable time, but if you want to play, by all means."

There was more to the admonishment than appeared on the surface, and I deserved the callout. Here I was, picking at him after I'd practically begged him to help. It wasn't him who I resented. It wasn't even Jolie.

It was myself.

I hated myself for getting involved when I'd been set on closure. The thing was, and I hadn't yet been able to admit it, I was beginning to realize I couldn't have closure without first getting involved.

So I needed to just fucking commit and stop being a dick about it. "We're cool. Let's get on with this."

"Great." He opened a drawer and pulled out a notepad wrapped in a pretentious executive style cover and dropped it on the desk. "What can you tell me, Jolie?"

She looked at me again, and I could read her question without her having to say it.

"You can trust him," I said, fully aware that her need to hear that meant she trusted *me*.

Ironic, wasn't it? That she had all the faith in me now that I'd wished she'd had back then. I didn't know how to feel about that, so I tried my best to pretend I didn't feel anything.

Thankfully, her attention was now on Donovan, so she couldn't see how badly I failed. "What is it you need?"

Donovan grabbed a gold-coated ballpoint pen from his front jacket pocket and removed the cap. "Information. Leads. I need to see where the opportunities are to find dirt on your father."

"What if what you find isn't enough to destroy him?"

"We'll make sure it does," Donovan assured.

Determined to play nice, I backed him up. "D has a knack for that as well."

"Seems you're a talented man." She practically purred, which was her way with people in general, but it made my hands bunch into fists all the same. "And you run a marketing firm? Why do I have a feeling you missed your calling?"

He pointed a finger to correct her. "I run an *international* marketing firm. But don't worry—I have plenty of other hobbies."

"I like this guy," she said with a wink.

"Don't." So much for playing nice.

"Can't help it."

"He's taken."

"That's not what she likes about me, Cade. Don't get your panties in a bunch." Wisely, he didn't give me a chance to bite back. "So opportunities for dirt—as you've likely realized by now, accusations of abuse aren't strong enough to do the kind of destruction we're looking for. Too much he said/she said involved, and there are statutes of limitations. We need something with meat—money laundering, theft, bribery, gambling, or a sex scandal could have potential. He hasn't happened to murder anyone, has he?"

"Um." She glanced at me as if to ask *Is he for real?* I nodded. "Not that I'm aware of."

"Too bad. That would be a nail in his coffin for sure." He jotted something down on his notepad. "Still might be something we could explore. Does he have any enemies?"

Okay, maybe I was looking for reasons to crap on his ideas now, but this had to be said. "We're not going to kill someone just to frame him. The whole reason we're here is to *not* kill someone."

"I wasn't suggesting that we kill anyone. Just, you know, some people end up dead all on their own."

I gave him a glare that I hoped he understood as *knock it off*.

Jolie didn't seem bothered by the exchange or by our attempts to out-piss each other. Or she was too busy considering options for destruction to really pay attention. "Isn't a sex scandal another he said/she said kind of thing?"

"You're correct there. But if there's any chance he's fucking minors... That would be a tough one to sell if it's not true, though, and you'll need a bunch of victims or hardcore evidence to pull it off." Her brow wrinkled, and he added, "Like bastard children. Semen on a blue dress from the Gap isn't going to get him more than a slap on the wrist."

Her lips twitched with a smile that couldn't quite force itself to form. "I guess that takes sex scandal off the list. Sad, isn't it? That fucking with people's money holds more weight than fucking with people's kids?"

Donovan grew gravely serious, which was saying something since the man was pretty serious in general. "It's not just sad, Jolie, it's disgusting. Which is why I have no qualms about creating a scandal from scratch, if need be."

"That's comforting." Another trusting glance toward me. "I think."

"It's this or murder," I said, laying down the facts. I didn't need to add that if she chose the latter, I was out.

She nodded. "I'm good with this."

"So tell me about him." Donovan propped his pen up, ready to write. "Who does he spend time with? Who are his friends? Who does he not seem to like? What are his hobbies? What does he do with his days off?"

Jolie chuckled. "Oh, is that all you want to know?"

"Sweetheart, that's only the beginning," he replied. "Better buckle in. It's going to be a long morning."

FIFTEEN

Two hours passed. Two hours of Donovan drilling for the particulars of Langdon Stark's life. Two hours where every one of Jolie's answers took me to a time in the past.

My short time at Stark's school had been completely unforgettable. I still remembered how the classrooms smelled. The sound of footsteps crossing the forbidden great hall remained distinct in my mind. Every encounter with Jolie—every stolen kiss, every shared dream—was etched permanently in my brain.

Or so I'd thought.

Now, as she sketched out the life of my once headmaster, events and details I'd neglected came rushing back. How had I forgotten Stark's weekly interstate private school committee meetings? Or that he'd liked to play Chopin's Death March during dinner? And that he imposed a "fine" for students who walked across the front lawn? (Students who weren't me, anyway. I got the beating plus the fine.)

There were new things I learned too. Family members of

Jolie's that I hadn't been aware of. Friendships I'd heard nothing about. Side projects that hadn't come about until after I'd left.

"How about his money?" Donovan asked as we entered our third hour. "Does all of it come from running the school?"

"About fucking time we got to something significant." For the most part, I'd stayed silent, letting Donovan decide what he needed to ask, but I was starting to get restless, and the walk down memory lane was taking a toll.

My partner glared, but neither he nor Jolie addressed me. "We have family money," she said. "The school was founded by my great-great-grandparents as a philanthropic endeavor. It wasn't intended to be the foundation of the family income, but every generation after them had at least one child that made it a primary focus. Since my father was an only child, it all rested on him."

More information I hadn't been aware of, which stemmed a new thought. "It will be yours one day."

This time she shifted to look at me. "It will."

I didn't know why it had never occurred to me. Is that where her loyalty had lain? With the school rather than her father? "Will you run it?"

"I was supposed to take over when he retired. But I won't step foot there as long as he's still around."

There was no way he would make any transition of power easy. He was not a man who stood idly in the wings, and I was surprised retirement had ever been discussed at all.

But if he stepped down, and she refused, who would run it then? Jolie was proud of the Stark contributions to education. I couldn't imagine her giving away the family legacy without a fight. Was that the reason behind her wanting her father gone?

The possibility had me softening toward her. Reluctantly.

"So your father has outside investments?" Donovan's tone made it clear he didn't appreciate the deviation from his line of questioning.

Jolie thought for a moment. "He must have. He never talked money with me, so I'm only guessing. He was very private about it."

"If he did have other investments, and if that was where his money truly came from, wouldn't it be odd that he still stayed so involved with the school? He could have handed it off to a board to run." Donovan tapped his pen against his notepad as he made each point.

"You mean, maybe we hadn't really been as wealthy as he made it seem? Maybe he relied on the income from the school?"

"I don't know. You tell me."

The man was good. He could have been a detective. Or an interrogator for the CIA. Or the mob.

"I never saw any indication that he was worried about money. There were never phone calls from collectors. There was never a concern about how often we ate steak. He spoiled me on occasion, and we always had nice things and went on nice vacations. Some years it did seem we might have had an influx of cash. We have a cabin in the woods that he bought out of the blue when I was ten, and he bought a beach house in Key West and a yacht when I was nineteen."

His eyes glinted as though he'd hit a jackpot. "Sounds like he definitely has access to other money. Running a private school doesn't buy you third homes and yachts, no matter how prestigious the place is."

"I really don't think this is going to lead you anywhere. I'm pretty sure we just had enough passed down to pay for all the extras." She paused, a flicker of doubt crossing her features. "I'd always assumed that, anyway."

"Possible. But then I'm back to questioning why he stayed personally involved at the school. Why not pay for someone else to do it and enjoy living life as a philanthropist? Does he enjoy being an educator?"

"I don't think he ever enjoyed anything besides being cruel," she said, and though she didn't look at me, it felt like a shared moment of honesty. No one knew her father's cruelty better than the two of us.

Donovan had spared me very little acknowledgement over the morning, but he looked at me now before replying. "Yes, Cade told me he was a sadist."

She fidgeted with the collar of her sweater. We'd never used that word outright. Donovan had been the first to say it to me, and of course that's what Langdon Stark was. It was odd having a term for it. It felt minimizing. Like he simply suffered from a personality disorder and wasn't really a malicious, inhumane monster.

No, he was still that. He would always be that. The word didn't take away his cruelty.

If Jolie found the term hard to reckon with, she didn't show it. "Kids find school torturous. Maybe that was enough for him to want to be hands on."

"Maybe so." Donovan wrote something down. Then, after a beat, wrote several more things down.

"Sorry I don't know more about his money."

"It's fine. I'll get my guy to look into it." He was still taking notes, preoccupied with his thoughts instead of us.

"Ferris won't have a problem with any of this?" I asked

when he'd been silent for a while. The PI had been on our payroll for years, but he'd been searching (unsuccessfully) for Jolie, not hacking into financial accounts. It might not be in his area of expertise.

Donovan didn't look up from his notepad. "We can't use Ferris. He's doing surveillance on someone else right now."

"On whom?" I'd only told him to drop the guy two days ago. What other job did he get him on since then? Something for the firm?

"Me, if you must know."

"He's doing surveillance on you? *For* us?"

"For Sabrina, actually." There was plenty to follow up with after that comment, but Donovan waved his hand like he was flicking away a bug. "Never mind that. I have someone else. Someone more suited to this type of work. He'll be able to track all his accounts and when money was put in and taken out. We'll have a better idea what we're looking at once he gets an initial report back to me." Finally, he returned his focus to the woman beside me. "You do realize this might take some time?"

She sat up straighter, and I could feel panic emitting off her. "How much time? I'm only in town until Friday."

"It's a long shot to say that we'll have what we need by then. Is this urgent?"

"I want it done as soon as possible."

My partner glanced toward me, and I took the cue. "I think he's asking if you're safe."

I felt my chest tense as I waited for the answer. I'd wanted to know about this since she'd first told me she wanted Stark dead, but she hadn't been forthcoming with her motives, and asking outright had felt somehow too personal.

Or maybe I was afraid of what she'd say.

"Oh. Yeah. I'm safe." Seeming to sense it wasn't enough assurance, she added, "My father doesn't know where I live. He hasn't been part of my life in ten years."

My muscles relaxed, and once again air flowed in and out of my lungs. She hadn't been ready to leave when I'd left, but seventeen years had passed. Of course she'd gotten away eventually.

But then my relief took on a new shape as I realized the implication of her statement. "Years? Is any of this information you've given today still accurate?"

"We don't need recent information to find something in the past." Donovan not only didn't seem to think it was a problem, he also didn't seem surprised.

I was already feeling pissy because of all the memories that had been drudged up and wasn't in any mood to realize Donovan had put things together that I'd missed. Adding to my annoyance was recognition that my knowledge of Jolie was hollow. There was so much I didn't know about her. So much of her life that I'd missed. So much of her life that she'd kept me out of.

I turned my wrath where it belonged—on her. "What are we even doing here, Julianna? If you haven't talked to him in years, then why do you suddenly—?"

She cut me off but addressed Donovan. "Do you have to know my reasons to make this happen?"

"I do not," the traitor said. "I just need to know what the time frame has to be. I'll push to have things happen as fast as possible, but no promises. And if safety becomes a concern, we'll want to rethink our plan."

"Sure. Thank you."

I shook my head, my fingernails digging into my palms,

wondering if I should think about hitting the boxing club again later.

Donovan turned unexpectedly to me. "Need to walk it off, Cade? You could take a trip to the vending machine if you need to blow off some of that hot energy. Weston still has that dartboard in his office, if you'd prefer."

I would prefer punching him in the jaw.

"I'm good." I gave him a forced smile. I wasn't about to let him look like he was the tough one, and fantasizing about kicking his ass was already calming me down.

"Glad to hear. We're nearly done anyway. Any other details you can tell me? Anything odd? Anything at all out of the ordinary ever happen at school or at home?"

"Um..." Jolie sighed, the first sign that this conversation was exhausting her as well. "Someone gave him a car once."

"*Gave* him a car?" His reaction suggested he thought this was something he might have been told earlier.

"Yeah. A Land Rover."

"A parent? A bribe for school entrance?"

"I don't know who gave it to him. I don't think it was a parent, but maybe. I don't know." She seemed flustered. Embarrassed maybe for not bringing it up before or for not having better answers.

"Definitely worth looking into." He made a note.

"Yeah, his wife wasn't too happy about it." She looked at me. I could feel her eyes even though I refused to look in her direction.

"I'll bet." He circled whatever he'd written before. "What else?"

"He owns a gun. He owns several guns for hunting, but he

always kept those at the cabin, and this one wasn't for hunting. It's a revolver."

"Legally registered?"

"I think so."

My entire body tensed at the thought of that man with a gun in his hand.

"When did he purchase it?"

"Uh, when..." She didn't want to say it, which told me everything.

"He got it when I left, right? He get it for me? In case I came back?"

She nodded, her mouth tight. "He keeps it in the night-stand by his bed. Or he did. I don't know if he still does."

"Loaded?" I asked, surprised at how calmly I was discussing a man wanting me dead.

"No, but the bullets are in the same drawer."

"Good to know," Donovan said, like we were talking about double A batteries instead of bullets. Like I hadn't just realized how close I'd come to probably losing my life. The number of times I'd considered going back, the number of times I'd actually started out in that direction...

I'd thought I was a coward for staying away. Turned out I'd also been smart.

But I'd left her in that house with that man and a gun.

I didn't want to think about that and was grateful Donovan took another road of thinking. "What did your mother die from, Jolie?"

"Not a gunshot. Brain aneurysm when I was four."

"You're sure that's what she died from and not just a story he told you?"

Her frown said that it had never occurred to her to question it. Hadn't occurred to me either.

"I'll have my guy follow that up too." He made a note. "Anything else?"

She shook her head, wrapping her arms around herself like a hug, and I wondered what she was feeling. She hadn't hated her father like I had. She hadn't liked him either, but her feelings toward him had been more complicated. While she'd never told me about the times she'd been punished, I was sure it had been abusive. But she hadn't gotten punished often. He'd also doted on her. Heaped her with praise. Treated her like a princess. They'd been close in a way I'd never been with my mother, despite the fact that I'd also grown up in a single-parent home.

I'd resented her for that. For having something I'd wanted and for not being able to hate the man the way I had.

What had I expected from her? To run off and leave him forever? What a fucking child I'd been.

What a fucking child I was.

Thinking of running away abruptly brought another thing I'd forgotten to mind. "There was that kid that went missing the year I was there. Bernard Arnold?"

"He was just a runaway," Jolie explained. "Not that unusual. Teens do that sometimes."

Donovan wasn't so dismissive. "He ran where? Back home?"

"No. Just away."

"They ever find him?"

"I'm not sure."

Once again, Donovan and I exchanged glances. It wasn't something I'd thought was suspicious before. Like Jolie had said, teens run away. I'd considered running away more than once.

He said what I was thinking. "Any chance he ran away because of your father? Is it possible he doled out punishment to him as well?"

"I guess." She didn't seem to buy it. "But for real—kids run away. It wasn't unusual. Two seniors took off when I was a freshman too."

Donovan opened his mouth, but already presuming he was going to ask for more information, she beat him to speaking. "Two girls. It's possible they had an altercation with my father, but the rumor was they were in love. It's more likely they ran off to be together."

This time I was the one boring my eyes into her, and she was the one who refused to look at me. "Huh. Who would have thought escaping was an option?"

She flinched but still wouldn't look at me. "And cruel as Daddy was with his mind games, I never once heard anyone mention anything about physical punishments. Other than Cade, I mean. And obviously he had reason and opportunity with Cade that he didn't have with others."

"You might not have been the girl kids shared that kind of rumor with," Donovan said bluntly. "Being his daughter and all."

I had a feeling she doubted that. She'd prided herself on being informed when it came to the student body. I'd always suspected it was one of the reasons she'd had the reputation with the boys that she'd had when I arrived on the scene. That rep had always bothered me, but I'd understood her motives. She'd wanted to be someone they could trust. She'd wanted to keep tabs on what her father might be doing to them. She'd wanted the attention to make her feel like someone cared.

But Donovan had a point.

"I never heard anything either," I volunteered.

"You might not have been considered a safe person either, all due respect."

Okay, that was another good point.

"Do you remember the girls' names? I'll check them out as well."

She rattled them off. Donovan jotted them down.

He was still looking at his notepad when he asked his next question. "You said he hasn't been part of your life in ten years. I'm assuming that's when you moved away?"

"Correct. I know my information isn't necessarily accurate anymore."

That wasn't where Donovan was going with his line of questioning. "He didn't *try* to keep in touch or you didn't *let* him?"

"I didn't tell him where I went. I found someone to give me a fake ID and was able to enroll in college under that name. Paid my own way with student loans."

I folded my arms over my chest, pretending this wasn't interesting to me in the slightest.

"And you've been using that identity since? You didn't legally change it?"

She shook her head. "I didn't want to be traceable."

"So now you live your life under the name Jolie?"

"Yeah."

"Jolie...what?"

I recognized what he was doing. He'd pushed me to have

Ferris look into her now that we knew where to look, and I'd resisted. Donovan could never resist knowing all, though.

But Jolie had never been a dummy. "Why are you focused on me all of a sudden? I haven't been in his life in a decade. I'm not going to be able to give you anything that I haven't already given you."

He produced his most innocent look, which wasn't very innocent at all, but managed to win over a surprising amount of people. "I'm only trying to see if there are opportunities surrounding your estrangement that you might not have thought about. It seems safe to assume that something occurred that made you decide to cut him off."

"He was a strict man who brought out a belt anytime the dishes weren't stacked correctly in the dishwasher. Does there have to be another reason?"

"There does not." Donovan knew when he'd met a wall.

I wasn't surprised by it. That was how she'd always been, whenever I tried to actually talk about what we were going through back then—cold and closed off. I'd had to put the pieces together about her father myself. I imagined she'd learned early that her father demanded perfection. She'd learned to always stack the dishes correctly before I ever met her. Without her giving him excuses to be punished, he had to look elsewhere.

To be fair, I'd gotten cold when she'd tried to get me to open up about it too. We lived it together. We didn't need to talk about it.

As perceptive as Donovan was about hitting barriers, he was also fond of trying to bulldoze through them. "But you were an adult. You weren't living with him anymore. Presumably he wasn't still punishing you for how you did the dishes."

If the answer to this related to her reasons for wanting her father gone, I expected she wouldn't respond.

But after a tense beat passed, she did, though reluctantly. "No. He wasn't."

"Then was there something that motivated your leaving?"

Her head shook, barely perceptible. "Delayed reaction, I guess." Another beat. "And if he *had* still been abusive, it wouldn't matter because, like you said earlier, he said/she said won't get us anywhere."

"I did say that."

"And you said you didn't need to know my reasons."

"I said that too." For a second, I thought he'd leave it alone. "But we might be able to use your leaving. Could blame it on something else. Say you discovered something he'd done. Were afraid for your life."

"Would that be helpful?" There was a raw note in her timbre that suggested saying she'd been afraid wouldn't have been a lie, and that bothered me more than I wanted to admit.

"I don't know yet." His intercom buzzed. "I need more information before I can tell you that." He put his phone on speaker. "This better be urgent, Simone."

"Sabrina says there's a client who's demanding to see Weston. She explained he wasn't available, and now he wants to see you."

Donovan rolled his eyes. "Tell her I'll be right there." He pressed the button to end the call. "How does Weston always draw out the crazies, even when he's not here?" He stood up and buttoned his jacket. "I should have enough to get us started. Sorry to run out like this. I'll be in touch."

He scurried out of the room, letting the door shut behind him.

We'd been dismissed, which was good because I'd officially reached a point where I couldn't hear anymore. It was hard enough grappling with the past shit that I'd been a part of. I didn't know where to begin processing the new revelations.

Had she been afraid?

I'd always believed he hadn't treated her as cruelly as he'd treated me. She'd learned how to live within the lines, or he was easier on her because she was a girl, or no one had ever made him as pissed as I had.

Truth was, I'd let myself believe that my leaving had to have calmed him down.

Wishful thinking, perhaps.

Self-centered, definitely.

My leaving also may have had the opposite effect. I'd taken away his favorite punching bag. Had she become my replacement?

The possibility nagged at me as I brought her coat to her and held it out for her to put on. Her brow rose in surprise. Then she stood and let me help her put it on, one arm, then the next.

The scent of blossoms infiltrated my senses, but I didn't step away. Even after her coat was on. Instead, I turned her around, and pulled the fur edges together to button her up.

"Did he get worse, Jolie? After I'd gone?" I'd whispered it, afraid that if I spoke too loudly, I would scare her truth away. That she'd turn cold on me too. I didn't even care that she'd heard me call her by that name. I was too anxious about the answer.

Her gaze locked onto mine, and she brought her hand up to cover my own. "You know he was never as hard on me as he was on you." Her voice was equally soft.

"That doesn't tell me anything."

"What do you want me to say? That he became a sweet, loving man the minute you left? He was still him. Quick with his tongue. Quicker with his hand."

Years of separation disappeared, and all the distance between us now was a few inches. Whatever shit had kept us apart felt insignificant in the moment. We had shared something that so few people were unfortunate enough to share. Lucky enough to share, too. Once we had been everything that mattered to each other. It had been the two of us against the world. Against him. That had bonded us in a way that couldn't be ignored, no matter what else had happened between us, and with that recognition, a sudden overwhelming wave of guilt washed over me as well.

"You should have come with me." I tugged her closer, holding her coat as though keeping her here now could have kept her with me then. "Even if you hadn't wanted to be with me. I would have gotten you out of there. I would have gotten you free."

Her breath stuttered as she drew in. "It wasn't your job to be my savior."

"But I wanted to be."

I had wanted to save her and fix her and give her safety and a life that was better, and as angry as I had tried to be with her for not letting me do those things, I also knew I hadn't fought hard enough. I'd failed her.

I didn't want to fail her again.

She reached her fingers up to brush across my cheek, her stroke burning into my skin with a welcome fire. "Cade...?"

I didn't know what she was asking, but I knew what she

needed. After all this time, I could read her body language like we'd invented it together.

I needed it too. Needed to feel her lips on mine. Needed to see if kissing her now held the magic and escape that kissing her then had.

I started to lean in.

And the door burst open. "Apparently, I need my wallet. This jackoff is expecting me to take him to lunch."

I jumped back from Jolie like she was forbidden. Old habits die hard. Donovan didn't make any indication that he knew what he'd interrupted, but he wasn't the kind of guy who missed anything. It was unusually generous for him not to gloat about it, considering our bet, so I tried to be generous in return. "Do you need me to step in?"

"I don't think it's an occasion for a heavy hand." He pulled his coat out of the closet and patted the pocket to be sure his wallet was there. "Sabrina is coming as well. It won't be all terrible. Especially if I can convince her to let me finger her under the table."

Knowing Donovan, Sabrina wouldn't really have a say.

"Sorry for the crass language," he said, remembering Jolie was there. "I'm in love."

As if that was an excuse.

He turned back to me. "Besides, you have a stack of performance reports to work on. Don't worry. I'll bring you something back."

I'd forgotten about the promise to help him.

It was a blessing, actually. Because then I could send Jolie away and lose myself in paperwork and ignore the feeling that I was once again about to lose myself in her.

SIXTEEN

Hours later, I closed the folder on the last performance report and pushed it aside. Donovan hadn't been lying when he'd said there'd been a stack of them. All of us preferred to keep what work we could digitized, but a stubborn portion of our clients still wanted a hardcopy printed and signed off on each quarter. These were the reports we tended to leave until the last minute possible. Weston had pushed them off, then left the contiguous United States.

When I'd still had quite a few to go through by the time Donovan was ready to leave the office, I'd piled the rest in a recycling shopping bag I'd found in the office kitchenette and taken them back to the hotel. A bigger man would have taken the project up to his room. Instead, I'd commandeered a table in the restaurant and both hoped and dreaded that Jolie would eventually come down for dinner.

It was close to ten, and she hadn't made an appearance. Did

that mean she'd gone somewhere else to eat or ordered room service?

Fuck. Why did I even care?

I scrubbed a hand over my face then picked up my phone to text Donovan. **Reports done. Should I bring them to you or the office?**

He didn't need them until the morning, but I could drop them off tonight. It would give me another excuse to avoid my hotel room, and since my skin started to buzz every time I thought about going up—every time I thought about *her*—it seemed like a good idea to try to make sure she was asleep before I returned.

Not that I was worried anything would happen with her.

I'd been seconds from kissing her earlier—and kissing her was one thousand percent not something I needed to be doing —but that had been a fluke of circumstances. We'd been talking about the past, and I'd been caught there. The idea of kissing her had seemed natural in the moment. It wasn't something I was still thinking about. It wasn't something I planned to think about ever again.

Still. Distance did seem prudent. In case *she* had other ideas.

I started to gather the reports to put in the bag when Donovan replied. **I sent someone to pick them up from your room.**

I couldn't get my fingers to type fast enough. **Too much trouble. I'll drop them off.**

It's already done.

Barely any time had gone by since I'd sent my first text. Surely there was time to reverse his orders.

But that would mean explaining to Donovan why I needed

an excuse to avoid my hotel room, and considering the bet we had going, there was no way he was going to support me. Probably why he'd sent someone in the first place. Because he wanted me alone with Jolie. Alone with no distractions. Alone with nothing to think about but each other.

I swallowed a groan and signaled the waitress over to close out my tab. If Donovan was sending one of his lackeys to my room, I'd better be up there to meet them.

Ten minutes later, I was standing outside my door, feeling déjà vu. Hadn't I done this whole get-myself-together-before-seeing-her routine last night? It was stupid and unnecessary. Without hesitating, I swiped my key card and pushed into the room.

Like the night before, I was met with the low murmur of a television set, but this time the TV was on in the living area. Apparently, the hotel staff had it switched out during the day, which meant there was no reason to give Jolie my room tonight, and the couch bed was already pulled out, so it seemed she was planning to sleep there. There was a half-eaten burger and salad on a tray on the desk, too, so I knew she'd been in for most of the night and that she'd gotten something to eat.

Only, she wasn't there now. A peek into my bedroom told me she wasn't there either.

Irrational panic ticked up the rate of my pulse. I dropped the bag and my coat on the floor by the couch and headed toward the only other room in the suite, the bathroom. I was halfway there when I realized the water was running.

She's here. She's fine. Just taking a shower.

As my heart calmed, I walked to the wall and banged my head against it. What the fuck was wrong with me? She'd said it herself—it wasn't my job to save her. And there was nothing to save her from here anyway. It had to be old instincts kicking in. That never-ending trepidation that had underscored every other emotion back in those days. *Be careful. Watch your back. Don't get too comfortable.*

It had been years before I'd felt any sort of peace. Nowadays, fear was foreign. Then as soon as Jolie was back in my life, I was right where I'd been at eighteen.

No. I refused. I was a different man now. She wasn't going to change that.

And I definitely wasn't going to think about the fact that she was currently down the hall naked.

The sound of knocking prevented me from exploring that last thought further.

I shouldn't have been surprised to see Simone standing there when I opened the suite door. "Daddy has you working overtime too?"

Simone was the type who could be dangerous—a provocative beauty with black frizzy hair and dark features who would do anything for Donovan Kincaid. She worshipped him, and not even necessarily in a sexual way. She just seemed to be into the kink of submission, with or without the sex, and since we'd made it a rule not to bang our subordinates, her relationship with her boss had gone without.

But he could get that woman to do anything without any fuss, including going to Midtown at ten o'clock at night to pick up a bunch of non-urgent performance reports.

Simone made a sultry harrumph sound and pushed past me into the suite. "I might have volunteered for the job." She peeked over her shoulder to see my reaction, batting her lashes, and now I understood her motives for volunteering went beyond pleasing her boss. "You barely looked at me today at the office, Cade Warren."

At the time it was made, the rule of not banging our subordinates had included not banging each other's subordinates, which was why Simone and I hadn't ever fooled around. She'd made it clear she'd been interested. Of course I'd been interested—I wasn't an idiot. But I'd been respectful of my partner and our agreement and had kept my hands off.

Now that Donovan was with Sabrina—who was Weston's subordinate—it seemed which subordinates were hands off had been redefined. And with Simone and I no longer working in the same office, all the obstacles that had prevented us from getting it on before had been removed.

Her body language said that she was fully aware our situation had changed.

Well, shit. That altered my plans for the rest of the night.

Except, actually, it didn't.

The flick of her tongue over her lips thing she was doing would have had me jumping last week. This week, the only lips on my mind belonged to the woman currently naked in my shower, and my cock had been sporting a semi before I'd even known who was at the door. It was possible that fucking Simone could help redirect my thoughts—an erection worked the same no matter where the inspiration came from—but banging Blondie the other night hadn't helped get my mind off Jolie. It was unlikely Simone would be any different.

I crossed to the bag, picked it up, and held it out for her to take. "I appreciate what you're offering, but it's not a good time."

Her mouth turned down into a pout. I'd expected that. I

hadn't expected her to reach out, ignore the bag, and lift the edge of my hoodie to get her hands underneath.

"Excuses, excuses. We should put all those aside for the night. It's the holidays. Give yourself a present." Now she was tugging at my belt. "Give me one too while you're at it."

"Oh, hey, no thanks." I tried to take a step back and bumped against the side of the sofa. "Really. This isn't hap—"

She cut me off with a kiss. At the same time she shoved a hand down my pants in search of my still semi-aroused manhood.

And of course that was exactly the second that Jolie would walk down the hall, her hair dripping wet, wearing nothing but a big, fluffy, complimentary hotel robe. "Oh. I didn't realize you had company."

Simone broke the kiss and stepped back, the additional person in the room apparently more motivating than my protests. "Whoops. I didn't mean to intrude." In true Simone fashion, she didn't sound all that sorry.

"I'm the one intruding, it seems." Jolie smiled, but her tone was bitter, and much as this whole situation sucked, I did like imagining the bitterness had something to do with jealousy. "I'd planned to sleep out here tonight, so if you'd like to move this to the bedroom... Or I can just grab my things and go in there myself. You won't even know I'm here."

"How modern-relationship," Simone quipped.

Before she started getting any ideas of how modern my supposed relationship with Jolie was, I shoved the bag of reports in Simone's hand. "Simone was just going." Glad she hadn't gotten around to taking her coat off yet, I turned her around and ushered her toward the door.

"I don't have to be going. I can be quiet." Her whisper was

loud enough for Jolie to hear, which made her argument less believable. "Or I can be loud, if that's what you prefer."

She winked, and suddenly I wasn't sure if she really had been coming on to me or if this had all been some sort of ploy set up by Donovan to stir trouble. I didn't put it past him, though I did question what his reasoning would be. Sending his drop-dead gorgeous secretary to seduce me in front of Jolie hardly seemed the best strategy for getting me to take my former lover to bed.

Whatever Simone/Donovan's objective had been, I could use it to my advantage. Let Jolie think she was in the way. Remind her I had every intention of keeping her at a distance. Motivate her to stay away.

If it also made her jealous, even better.

"Sorry, sweetheart," I said as I opened the door. "I'm trying to be a good roommate. Next time I'm in town, okay?"

"Don't change your plans because of me," Jolie called from behind me. "I have earbuds."

There went the jealous-ex-girlfriend vibe I'd been digging.

Simone trailed a single finger down my chest. "We could have a good time..."

"Go." I practically pushed her into the hall. "Thank you for coming by. It's always nice to see you, Simone. Good night."

I didn't let her respond, pulling the door shut and letting out a deep breath when the lock clicked in place.

"You both seemed cozy."

I turned to find Jolie bent over her suitcase, searching for something in the contents. She wasn't even looking at me, as though the preceding incident had not only not bothered her, it also hadn't deserved her interest.

The sharp edge in her tone said otherwise.

Jealous-ex-girlfriend vibe was back in full force.

"We've worked together. That's all." I played it cool, toeing off my shoes, making myself comfortable.

"You invited her to your hotel room. It seems there was definitely more to it than that."

Of course she hadn't realized that we hadn't come back to the suite together. I'd parted with Jolie hours ago, staying at the office to work. It probably looked like I'd spent the rest of the day and evening with Simone.

I had no reason to correct that assumption. "I suppose I wasn't thinking. Forgot I wasn't rooming alone. I don't usually have to worry about that."

She stood up. The T-shirt she'd stolen from me was clutched in one hand, a pair of flimsy see-through panties in the other.

Fuck. Now I was thinking about those panties. And the fact she wasn't wearing any underneath that big fluffy robe. My cock jerked to attention.

Good thing it wasn't my cock making decisions around here. His reaction was definitely my signal to call it a night.

Or maybe take a shower myself. Temperature set to cold.

I was already headed toward the bathroom when Jolie stopped me. "You know, Cade..." She sounded tentative. "I understand you are used to living a certain kind of lifestyle."

Certain kind of lifestyle? Was she calling me a manwhore? I was intrigued enough to turn around and face her.

"And I realize that having me here is probably getting in the way of that lifestyle." She paused.

"Go on."

Hesitantly, she approached me, her cheeks rosy, her lips wet. "If you really need to...you know. I don't have to be an inconvenience. I'm here. You're here. There's no reason I couldn't help out with...your needs."

I blinked incredulously, not sure she was talking about what I thought she was talking about but unable to figure out what else she could possibly mean. "I'm fine. Thanks."

She eyed the bulge in my jeans. "You sure about that?"

Okay then. She was definitely talking about what I thought she was talking about.

I choked back a laugh. "Uh, no. Definitely not."

She took another step toward me. Now we were close enough that I could feel her exhale. "Why not? I'm a woman, you're a man. No-strings hookups seem to be your M.O. Me being here is preventing you from going after that. Might as well be useful."

Any other beautiful woman saying those words to me, and I'd be stripping already.

Those words coming from Jolie made me wince. She was not my usual M.O. She was not disposable. Or forgettable. She was not string-free.

How could she even consider putting *me* in that box?

Still, I was trapped in place. Glued to the spot. She placed her hand on my chest, and even through the hoodie, my skin scorched.

"Stop it," I warned, my restraint thinning.

"Hell, it could be fun. Everyone wants a night with an ex-lover, don't they?"

"No fucking way." I wasn't even thinking about the bet with Donovan. It was a matter of self-preservation.

"Because we're not strangers? After all these years, we kind of are. That's your type, right? Someone you don't know? Or is it because you can't separate now from the past?"

All my blood was running south, but I managed to come up with a decent argument. "How about because you think that sex equals love? Is that reason good enough?"

"Ouch." She blanched and moved away. Only one step, but her heat went with her, and she suddenly felt a mile away. "That was a lot of years ago, you know. I'm sure your innocence has faded too. You probably don't still think love can save the day, for example."

It stung more than it should have, which was fair since I'd set out to hurt her first. It angered me that she could still understand me so well, and I'd lashed out. I didn't really believe she was still that naive. I certainly wasn't.

But that was who she'd been when I'd met her—a girl seeking affection in whatever way she could get it. She'd been the school's official boy toy when I'd transferred in, and while I was pretty sure she hadn't slept with most of her conquests, she'd been on her knees enough to make it a sore spot to my ego. Particularly when I'd never been one of the boys who'd been lucky enough to receive one of Julianna Stark's famous blow jobs.

I hadn't really wanted that from her then. I'd wanted to be special to her. I'd wanted to treat *her* special. I'd wanted to give her more than praise spouted out in a moment of fleeting euphoria.

For all the good it did. Here we were, strangers, like she'd said. I wasn't special to her.

She didn't have to be special to me.

And hadn't I earned a turn with her on her knees?

She must have read my thoughts because she stepped forward, and now she was close again. "Look. It doesn't have to be a big deal." She fingered the button of my jeans, but unlike when Simone had her hands in the vicinity, this time my cock reacted.

"I'm not asking you to do this." I put my hand on her wrist, meaning to push her away, but instead just stilling her.

"You're not asking. I'm offering. With all you're doing for me, I owe you this. I think you need it. Let me give it to you."

Everything she said pissed me off.

Worse, it turned me on. Made me unimaginably hard. Made my thinking originate from my little head instead of my big. She wanted me to treat her like those boys had? She wanted to minimize everything that had been between us with something transactional? She wanted to feel cheap? She wanted to be used?

Fine. I could do that.

I could use the hell out of her and feel fucking good about doing it too.

SEVENTEEN

"**K**neel down." The order flew from my mouth, harsh and impossible to disobey.

Jolie's pupils got wide and dark. The surprise, I understood. I hadn't been like that with her before. Back then, I'd been sweet and adoring and nice. Forceful tones had been part of our every day. There'd been no place for them in our lovemaking.

But this wasn't about love. This wasn't about nice. This was about justice. And closure. And basic, primal need, and the lust present in her dilated eyes said that maybe somehow this was meeting a need for her too.

"I'm not saying it again, Jolie. Get on your knees."

She fell to the ground instantly, her mouth open and waiting before I had to ask. I didn't want to think about all the boys who'd seen her like this back at school. I didn't want to think about any men who'd seen her like this after I'd left, but I forced myself to be aware of them all the same. *You're not special. You are one of a crowd.*

The acknowledgment made me even harder. Made me more desperate than ever to have my piece. My belt was still undone from Simone, so all I had to do was pop the button and unzip my fly, but I paused before I pushed my jeans down. "One more thing I need to make clear."

She nodded eagerly, and I wondered if she'd still be nodding when I said what I had to say. "This is for me, not for you. Got it?"

Her lips curled into a smile. "I didn't expect it would be any other way."

A sharp stab of pain shot through my chest until I shoved it aside and made myself stone. This was what we were now. This was all we could be.

With that settled, I pushed my jeans and underwear down together, just far enough for my cock to spring free and in her face.

Her breath drew in audibly. I hadn't reached my full potential by the age of eighteen. I'd had a significant growth spurt after I'd last been with her, and my cock had gone from a very normal width and length to a size that most called impressive.

I could sense the compliment on her tongue, and though I normally liked hearing it, I didn't want it from her. I was feeling mean and contemptuous. I didn't want her praise. I didn't want her awe. I wanted to shove my impressive cock so far down her throat that she couldn't breathe.

So before she could get out a single syllable, I was pushing my crown between her lips and into her lush mouth.

Fuck. Her mouth. Damp and hot. Heaven.

I'd planned to get in, fuck hard, and get right back out, but her tongue curled around my length as I pressed in, sending a storm of sensation down my spine. I closed my eyes and paused my stroke, trying to get my bearings before I exploded.

In my hesitation, she took over, wrapping her small hand around the base of my cock. Then she moved her mouth over me, sucking me in as far as she could before releasing me to the tip. Again. Again. Long, hard sucks that had me shivering.

After three trips up and down my cock, she swirled her tongue around my head, then started the whole pattern over again, bringing me closer to the edge on each round. Bringing me closer to erupting.

Bringing me dangerously close to losing my mind.

I closed my eyes hoping it would help. If I didn't see her, I could pretend I didn't know her. That she was a woman I'd just met in the bar. That I could get lost in the selfishness of pleasure and forget everything else between us.

But there wasn't any real forgetting.

Even if she had been another woman on her knees, it would still be her face in front of me, plastered on the back of my eyelids. Because it was always Jolie I thought of, even when I didn't acknowledge it to myself. She was always the undercurrent of every sexual encounter.

And even if she wasn't always the undercurrent of my sexual encounters, I wouldn't be able to pretend now. She felt familiar, despite never having taken me like this. The way she touched me, the sounds she made as she sucked me off, the smell of her own arousal wafting up to my nose—they were uniquely her, and there was no way not to feel a tug of emotion with each draw of her lips against my sensitive skin.

My world suddenly felt like it was spinning, and I urgently looked for something to steady me. My hands fell on her head, tangled in her hair, pulled at it from the roots. I opened my eyes, and they immediately crashed into hers. Green-rimmed pools of beauty held my gaze, probing me with intensity as she worked her jaw over my cock.

I hated her.

In that moment, I realized just how much I did. How much I had for years. I hated her for hurting me, and for letting herself be hurt, and for hiding, and for having the guts to face me again after all this time. I hated her for throwing away what we'd been and for not allowing us to find out what more we could be.

I hated her for not loving me enough.

I hated her because I'd loved her too much.

A blast of fury spread through my torso. I braced her face with my hands, holding her still so I could control the speed and depth of my next thrust. She didn't fight me. Her jaw went slack. Her eyes looked at me with something akin to trust.

"Did you learn this from them?" I drove in until my tip touched the back of her throat, barely letting her breathe when I pulled out before thrusting back in. "Birch and Wesley and Troy? Did they teach you how to take a cock like this?"

Her eyes watered, but the hitch in her breath made me wonder if the shaming aroused her.

I didn't want her to enjoy this, but the possibility that she did somehow made me even harder. I looked for more signs of pleasure. Besides her dilated eyes, her skin was flushed and splotchy. Her chest rose and fell with rapid breaths.

"Open your robe," I demanded.

She did without question, exposing plump breasts, and it was my turn to suck in a breath. I hadn't been the only one who'd had a growth spurt after high school. Before, she'd perfectly fit my palm. I didn't move my hands to be sure, but it looked like she'd spill over if I groped her now.

More provoking than the sight of her beautiful tits was the steepled nipples they sported. Two solid beehives, begging to be touched and sucked and pulled. Proving that her body was reacting to this blatant exploitation. Inviting me to use her in other ways. Inviting me to use her all night long.

I could do that. Easily. Could pull her up to her feet, kiss her until her knees buckled. Carry her to the other room and make her come a thousand different ways until morning.

But if I did, it would mean something.

Not because I couldn't separate the present from the past, but because in the present, I still loved her as much as I hated her. Nothing I did would ever change that. It was a commitment I'd made at the age of eighteen, and maybe Headmaster Stark had turned me into a masochist because I'd stuck miserably by that commitment for seventeen years.

There would never be closure. Not with Jolie.

Frustration threatened to distract me from orgasm, but one more glance at her face—tears streaming down her cheeks, her jaw struggling to take me all in—and I was almost there. Electric shocks ran down my cock and up my spine, radiated from my limbs. My torso spasmed like I'd been tickled. Two more pumps, and I was going to come.

And as much as I wanted her to suck me dry, that felt too good for her. Too intimate. She didn't deserve any more parts of me than she already owned.

Abruptly, I pulled out, wrapped my hand around my cock, and aimed at her breasts. As soon as she understood what I wanted, she stuck her chest out like it was an offering. Inviting me to defile her.

Three and a half strokes later, I was spurting white ropes across her tits, decorating her flushed skin with my cum as my body stuttered out my release. I grunted out a long curse word, adding way more vowels than normal. I forced my eyes to stay open, forced myself to memorize her like this—debased and dishonored and degraded.

"Feel better?" She sounded proud of herself, but not smug. Her smile seemed genuine. She stood up and pulled her robe back over her shoulders, leaving it open in front, probably so the garment wouldn't get dirty, but also giving me the advantage of seeing my artwork.

I thought about it a second. Actually, I *did* feel better. In the way that only a good orgasm could make me feel. Staring at the evidence of my release, my cock was already getting thick again.

And that made me not feel better anymore.

Because the fact was there was no end to this wanting. All these years, I'd told myself that if I just saw her again, if I just spoke to her, if I just knew how things had turned out then I could move on.

But I'd always known that was a lie. I would always want her. I would never be satisfied with just pieces. I would always want as much of her as she had of me.

And the real hitch of it all was that, even if she did say she wanted me too, I'd never be able to trust it.

It was a Catch-22. My own personal hell loop. One I was meant to suffer through alone.

I tucked myself away and pulled up my pants, not bothering to zip. "You need a wash rag to clean up?" I nodded toward the semen on her chest, but I didn't really look at her. I was already gone. My mind already safely shut behind the door to the bedroom with a couple of bottles from the minibar, ready to push her out of my mind and my heart with alcohol like I had so often over the years.

"I'll take another shower, if that's cool with you." Her tone was flat. Whether that was because I was listening to her from a distance or because she was disappointed that I was pulling away, I didn't know. I didn't care. It didn't matter.

What mattered was leaving the room.

"Good. That's a great idea. It's been a long day. I'm going to hit the sack now." I didn't listen for her response. I grabbed the liquor from the fridge and headed to my room, refusing to feel bad for making her sleep on the couch bed, or for leaving her a mess in my cum, or for not returning the favor.

There was only one thought of her I allowed myself as I disappeared behind a closed door and pushed her from my thoughts entirely: *See, Jolie. You're not the only one who can walk away.*

EIGHTEEN

I was used to waking up with morning wood and lingering dreams of Jolie.

I wasn't used to waking up that way with her in the next room.

It took a moment for the thought to register, but as soon as it did, I sat up straight and cursed.

Then I remembered what had happened the night before, and I cursed again.

What the fuck had I been thinking?

That's the thing—I *hadn't* been thinking. Now that I was thinking, I had a half-mile list of reasons why what had happened last night shouldn't have happened, starting and ending with *she was Jolie.* I couldn't even entertain it not mattering. Couldn't think for even a second, *is it really such a bad thing?* because every fiber of my being knew just how bad it was.

And also the reasons that it was so bad were not reasons I wanted to dwell on.

I needed closure for a reason—and in the daylight, I was no longer willing to believe that goal was impossible. Getting sucked off and jizzing all over her chest like I was marking my territory, though, was not very closure-esque.

I scrubbed a hand down my face. What was today? Tuesday? Three fucking days until she was out of here.

Three fucking days of trying to convince myself I didn't want to do a whole bunch of other bad things with her.

I grabbed my cell off the nightstand, scanned my email and messages, then not seeing what I was hoping for, called Donovan. "Any leads yet?"

"It's been one day, Cade." He sounded like that father who was tired from yelling every time his kids asked *are we there yet?*

To be fair, he sounded like that a lot when I called. "It should be a compliment that I think you can work so fast."

"Funny how your version of a compliment seems an awful lot like harassment." His voice got muffled like he'd turned his phone into his shoulder, but I could still make out what he said. "Is that still scheduled for ten thirty? Better make it ten forty-five."

I should have been sympathetic about his workload when I was sitting on my ass, shut behind a door, afraid of the woman on the other side.

But really all it made me feel was annoyed. "Is there something I can do to make things move along faster?" I'd even do more ad performance reports if it meant he'd get something concrete sooner.

I decided not to offer that specifically.

The muffled sound went away. "There is nothing you can do. There are things in motion. All we can do now is sit and wait for information to come in."

Pretty much what I'd expected, but not at all what I'd wanted to hear.

"What you're telling me is that twenty-four hours have passed, and you've got nothing?" Being irritated at Donovan was a lot more satisfying than being irritated by the situation.

"No, that is not at all what I'm saying. Hold on, no, Simone. I changed my mind. Move the Pritzogram meeting to after lunch, and then put the call with Dyson on at ten forty-five." This time he hadn't even bothered to mute me.

Obviously, he was busy.

Obviously, I didn't care. "So tell me what you found. I'll follow up."

I heard a door shut—his office door? Then he sighed. "There is nothing for you to follow up with, Cade. I gave the info to my guy as soon as I got back from lunch yesterday. Then I stayed up last night looking into a few things myself. Discovered a couple of other things for my guy to research—some out of the norm purchases, a pattern of runaways, etc., etc.—and as soon as he finds a single bit of useful information, he will get back to me, and I will get back to you. You get how that works? *I* call *you*. There wasn't a part of that scenario where you call me."

When Donovan got patronizing, it was time to hang up. Or punch him, but there was the whole we weren't near each other thing, and violence wasn't a real motivator where D was concerned.

But he'd said something I couldn't let slide. "A pattern of runaways? What's that supposed to mean?"

"Right now, it means exactly what Jolie said yesterday—teens run away. Ninety-nine percent of teens who do return home, even when abuse is involved, which is often. So even if Stark had pulled his shit with other kids, they would fit into the statistical data. Problem is, of all the runaways that have been reported at Stark Academy, I can only find one that's shown up again, and that's you."

Shit.

But data could be skewed. "Technically, I disappeared for a long fucking time too."

"I'm sure none of the other runaways shared your unique circumstances." He cleared his throat, and now he sounded like he was in motion, walking to his desk maybe. "Point is, it's unusual, and it's being looked into, and I will get you something eventually. Now's the part where you leave me alone and let that happen."

"Fine, fine. Fine." What other reaction could I have?

But that left me with nothing to do and a woman I needed to avoid in the next room. "I'll come by the office then to work. Put me on something to help with Weston being gone."

"Don't come in. Anything I have for you to do, I'd have to explain first, and that will take more time than just doing it. If you're here, you'll be in the way."

I resented that comment, but I'd have said the same thing if he tried to show up at the Tokyo office and help out, and he'd only been gone from there for six months.

Through the door, I heard the sofa bed creak. Then creak again. Jolie was awake, and panic returned. "What the hell am I supposed to do with her in the meantime?"

I could practically hear his smirk. "Holed up in a hotel room together? I'm sure you'll think of something."

I hung up with more cursing. *Fucking prick*. Was that why he didn't want me in the office? Was he withholding shit just to try to make his odds better on that stupid bet?

The only reason I didn't truly believe that was the case was because Donovan was too cocky to think his wagers needed interference. And to back up his point, he'd almost won last night.

Or, wait—*had* he won? Did BJs count as fucking?

Since we hadn't defined terms, I decided only fucking counted as fucking, which meant I hadn't lost, and I was resolved *not* to lose.

But I was also realistic—the two of us holed up in a hotel room together really wasn't working in my favor.

I leaned my head against the headboard, half listening as Jolie moved around the suite. The water turned on at the mini-bar. Making coffee, probably. The volume on the TV was turned up. The *Friends* theme song played.

The other half of my brain tried to remember back to when I was ten, and we'd moved to Poughkeepsie with Stan, my mother's boyfriend of the moment. Stan had been one of the more decent father figures in my life, which meant he didn't just ignore me or keep me locked in a bedroom all the time. It also meant he sometimes took me to the movies or let me go on day trips with the neighbor kids.

One such winter trip stuck in my head.

I picked up my phone and scrolled through a few things. Checked out my options.

Then I pulled on yesterday's jeans and a Henley from one of the dresser drawers and forced myself out of the bedroom.

As soon as I saw her, curled up in her panties and my T-shirt with a mug of black coffee in front of the television, I realized I should have taken a moment to prepare myself for being in her presence. Were we going to act like last night didn't happen? How was I planning to deal with the fact that every time I looked at her mouth, my dick got hard?

Fortunately, she decided the first answer for us. "Hey," she said, barely glancing at me before returning her gaze to her show. "There's still a pod of coffee if you want me to make some for you. Housekeeping only left two that aren't decaf, and I'm already drinking this one."

Normal then. We'd act normal.

"I got it. Thanks." Except this wasn't normal because there was no way I'd be making hotel coffee, and here I was, adding water to the machine. I peered warily at her like she was an unpredictable dog, one that I had to keep tabs on in case she suddenly decided to bite.

That wasn't fair.

So far, I'd been the one who'd done all the biting. She'd been perfectly nice. Nicer than necessary.

And now I was thinking about her on her knees again.

I forced my head in another direction. "So, uh, talked to Donovan. He's working on a few leads, but it's going to be a few days."

She didn't blink. "I figured."

"You planning on doing anything today?"

"Considering that I have two hundred fifty left in my account—that will probably pay for my meals this week with just enough left for the car ride to the airport—no. No plans." Abruptly, she turned her attention to me, as though she just realized I might be trying to get rid of her. "Do you need me to get out of your hair? I can find something to keep me occupied outside the room."

She started to stand up, but I waved her to stay put. "No, no. I wasn't getting at that." I concentrated on the task of coffee making, wondering why it was so hard to extend a simple invitation.

She seemed to sense I had more to say. "Do you need to go into the office? I'll be fine here alone if that's what you're worried about."

Come on, you pussy. Just fucking say it.

I turned to her. "Actually, I was thinking... Donovan doesn't need anything more from us, and sitting around here all day's just gonna make me stir-crazy. I don't know about you, but, um. We should just forget all the shit going on. For the day. Get out of here. Do something fun."

She looked at me in that way of hers, the way I'd never forgotten, where she made me feel like I was the only person that mattered on the planet. "Did you have something in mind?"

She wasn't flirting, really. Wasn't trying to be suggestive at all, and probably most definitely wasn't thinking about being spread out on that sofa bed so I could eat her like a breakfast buffet, so I made myself ignore the fantasy that had just popped in my head and focused on the idea I'd had when I brought the whole thing up. "Yeah. I think I do."

"Awesome. I'm game." Without even knowing what I had in mind, she was on board. Like she trusted me.

I had to not let myself think about that too long. "Cool. Dress warm."

I abandoned the tasteless coffee—we could pick up to-go in the hotel lobby on our way out—and went back in the bedroom so I could shoot Donovan a text. **I'm going to need to borrow your car.**

NINETEEN

An hour later, we were in Donovan's Jag, headed out of the city, and surprisingly, considering the fact that I hadn't been behind a wheel in years, I was managing the New York City traffic without any problems.

Donovan's threat to cut off my dick if I returned his car harmed in any way might have had something to do with my attentiveness.

Fortunately, concentrating on the task at hand made a good excuse for silence, but thirty minutes into the trip, we turned on I-87, and from there it was smooth sailing.

After that, the quiet between us might not have been awkward, but it did give me time to think, and the things my mind kept wanting to think about were complicated and heavy. Our past. Stark's future. Jolie's eyes. Jolie's lips.

Several times I found myself thinking about the night before, and not just the dirty parts, but the haunting parts. *You probably don't still think love can save the day,* she'd said. *You can't separate now from the past,* she'd said. *Because we're not strangers? After all these years, we kind of are.*

The last one was the one that tormented me most. Probably because it was the accusation that I felt I had the most control over. We were strangers, but we didn't have to be. We were strangers, but I could do something to change that.

Getting to know her might have seemed a counterintuitive way to go about getting closure, but in reality, not knowing her anymore was one of the things that stung the most about the status of our relationship. I used to know all of her. I'd wanted to know all of her for a lifetime. I'd planned on loving all of her forever.

Trying to hold her over the years had been like holding sand. Every day, some part of her slipped away, which had made me even more desperate to hold on to the parts of her that I still had.

So maybe if I didn't feel like I was clutching onto scraps, I could finally relax, open my fingers, and let her go.

Or maybe I'd just have more to clutch onto. Fuck if I knew. But it was as good of a plan as any.

I tapped the button on the steering wheel that adjusted the radio volume, and the You + Me Spotify list she'd turned on faded to background noise. She looked at me expectantly, assuming I must have something I wanted to say.

I really should have figured out what that was exactly before I'd turned down the sound. "You, um. You said we're strangers. It's weird. Thinking of you as a stranger."

Fantastic preface, asswipe. I was a bumbling teenager again, with absolutely no chill.

The corners of her mouth lowered, and she turned her

head to look out the window. "That's my fault. I know that wasn't fair to you."

"That wasn't what." I glanced at the back of her head and resisted the urge to touch her to try to get her to look back. "I wasn't trying to place blame. I was saying that, um." Why was it so hard to have an honest conversation with her? "I'm saying I don't like it."

"Oh." She turned her face back to study me, again in that way that made me feel like I was everything. "I don't like it either," she said, and it felt like she was making a confession. As though she wasn't sure she had the right to feel that way.

I wasn't sure she had the right either.

But I was glad she didn't like it.

With both of us on the same page, conversation should have flowed easily from there. Yet a whole song had started and finished before either of us spoke again.

"I'm a teacher," she said.

"You are?" I'd been handed gold. That little bit of information, tiny and miniscule in the wording, filled an entire quadrant of the Jolie puzzle. From this, I could envision the structure of her days. Could see the makeup of her years. I could begin to imagine the pattern of her life that had for so long seemed like a deep black, shapeless sea.

"Yeah." She gave me her best smile, and I knew now that she also liked the job. "Middle school literary arts. But I've taught high school too. And filled in for the assistant principal for a semester while he was having back surgery. My bachelor's is in secondary education English, but my master's is in educational leadership and policy."

"So you could one day take over the academy?"

She nodded without really committing. "I mean, it was

always in the back of my mind. Also, it just seemed like the most natural thing for me to do. Kind of in my blood."

"Yeah." When we'd been kids, we'd been so hell-bent on leaving everything behind that I'd never considered she'd follow the career path of her ancestors.

It made sense. From a practical, adult perspective, of course it did, and I was happy for her for finding her place like that.

But was it really her place? Or was it just a trap?

She had to know what I was thinking. "It was half the reason I hesitated too, Cade. I didn't want to have anything to do with the family legacy. I didn't want..." She shook her head, changing her course. "I didn't even go to college until I was twenty-five."

"Not really typical of a Stark alum." The academy promotional material bragged endlessly about the high percentage of graduates who pursued higher education.

"Not at all typical. I was proud of that. It felt rebellious, throwing away my potential and such." She picked up her phone from her lap and paused the playlist altogether. "Then I realized that throwing away my potential hurt me more than it hurt Daddy, and I was already working at the school so what was the point of avoiding it?"

"You *worked* at the academy?"

"I did. For a handful of years. Administrative stuff, mostly. Substitute teacher. Daddy didn't think a degree was necessary when the school was in the family. I didn't need any credentials. I was already hired. Which is bullshit, by the way, because you most certainly need credentials to run a school. But. Well. You know Daddy."

I did. But I didn't know what method he'd used to bully her into doing his bidding. Was it emotional and psychological manipulation? That seemed to be his favorite tactic with Jolie. Or had he resorted to physical abuse? She would have been an adult, but I doubted that would have stopped him from striking her if he'd thought it would be effective.

It was tricky wanting to know the present while having to dance around the past. It wasn't that her father or our time together was necessarily off limits, but I knew that if we went there, there was no coming back, and I wasn't sure that was a trip I wanted to take.

So I didn't ask the questions I wanted to ask and resigned myself to being content with what she chose to share on her own.

"When I finally decided to get a degree, I wasn't planning to ever go back to Stark Academy. But I kept returning to the education courses in the catalog. Like I said—it's in my blood. So I thought I'd try it until something else stole my interest, and no one else ever did."

My heart missed a beat.

I glanced at her and saw her cheeks pinken. "*Nothing* else ever did, I mean."

But now I wanted to know about her slip. Had she said that for a reason? Had there really been no one over the years? That couldn't be possible.

It would have been easy enough to ask. Natural, too. That was exactly the kind of thing a person asked about when catching up.

But I couldn't get myself to form the words, and then she was talking again. "I took a vacation week to come here. I don't have to be back until Monday, but I booked my flight for Friday because I thought I might need a couple of days after being here to..." *Recover.* She didn't have to fill in the blank. "There's only one more week before winter break, and I have more vacation. I could call in if we need more time. My lesson plans are already done."

No one else.

I could feel her eyes on me, waiting for an answer. "I think we need to wait until Donovan comes back to us before we think about that."

"Right. Sure." A beat passed, and I wondered if she knew what I was thinking. *No one else. No one else.* "What about you?"

There'd been no one else for me. Not anyone that I'd loved. Fucked, yes. Fucking wasn't the same.

But she couldn't be asking about that. What had she said before? "I'm one of the owners of my company. I get all the vacation I want."

She chuckled. "I meant..." She paused, as though trying to decide what exactly it was she meant. Then twisted in her seat to better face me. "How did you get involved with Donovan Kincaid?"

"He recruited me from, uh..." This wasn't necessarily safer ground. It would be if I stuck to my lie, the one I told most often when other people asked this question, but this was Jolie.

And I meant it about not wanting us to be strangers.

I went with the truth. "From dealing art. Forged art."

"Oh." My answer had startled her, but when she processed it, she had no judgment in her expression. "How do you get into a business like that? I'm sure there's not an application."

"You meet someone who knows a guy who knows another guy. I started out legit. Got a degree in international finance management. I was good at math in..." I didn't need to tell her my best subjects from school. "Well, you know. There's a lot of boring ways to use math, but I thought international would be an opportunity to get out of the country. But you can't really get anywhere without a master's, and when I graduated with my bachelor's, I had more student loan debt than I could afford, so when a guy I knew said he had a line on how to make some cash, I took the job."

"What did you do exactly? You didn't forge the art."

I laughed. We both knew I didn't have an artistic bone in my body.

But I also wasn't really interested in going into the specifics of what I'd done in the early days. The people I'd beat up. The ways I'd threatened men who got in our way. "Mostly, I was just there to look scary."

"I never thought of you as looking scary back in high school."

"Well, that's why I was intent on bulking up. I wanted to look scary." I'd been a scrawny teen who'd gotten his height before his width. I might have had a chance with Headmaster Stark if I'd looked like I did now.

She nodded, and I knew she understood.

"And you don't usually get to looking scary without actually *being* scary. I learned to fight. I can throw a pretty big guy around if necessary. I can also get someone to stay in line with just a look."

"No, you can't. Show me."

I tried for a full thirty seconds before giving up. "I can't do it." Even if I could stop smiling, I couldn't give "the look" on demand. Too bad because there were a shit ton of people I wished could have seen it from me. I'd imagined giving it plenty of times to the boys back at school. To her father. To her, sometimes. When I was feeling really bitter.

I wasn't feeling that bitter at the moment.

She squinted her eyes and studied me all the same. "Okay, I see it. You're...intimidating."

"Damn right I am. I'm also good at orchestrating people, it seems, so I moved up from heavy to management, and that's where I met Donovan."

"He was working management in illegal art? Or was he buying it?"

This was a detail I'd never been able to quite hammer out. "Not quite sure what his role was. Nate hooked us up. He's one of the other Reach owners. He was dealing art at the time, and when I got bumped up to the more civilized level of the business, our paths would cross now and again. Sometimes we'd go out drinking, get in trouble, or whatever, and this one night he brought along Donovan. Rich motherfucker, fresh out of Harvard with his MBA and fascinated with business strategy and structure, no matter what the field. Nate and I spent all night telling him about our jobs. Which was really bad judgment. We were lucky he wasn't an undercover because we told him everything."

"Why would you do that?"

I shrugged. "A lot of drugs and alcohol. And also Donovan has a way, if you haven't noticed."

"Oh, I've noticed."

Her tone made my chest tight with jealousy, and I both wanted to drill her about all the things she'd "noticed" about my asshole friend and also drive straight to the office and show Donovan "the look" and also maybe kick him in the nuts.

After a calming breath, I could live with doing neither. "It was a good thing we told him, in the end, because we impressed him. He told us both that he wanted to put something together eventually, some sort of business, and said he'd be back in a few years with an offer. Promised he'd have something to get me out of the States. Nate blew him off—he was too happy making money the way he was, though if you ask him about it now, he doesn't even remember the conversation. I thought it sounded like a nice way to eventually retire, and if he could get me someplace foreign, all the better. I still had a bunch of loans—I was making good money, but you don't want to pay off anything all in one bunch like that if the income isn't going to be reported on your taxes—but I was able to get them deferred and applied for more so I could get a master's in entrepreneurship. I wanted to be ready when he came back."

"You quit the other stuff just on this guy's maybe-someday offer?"

"Oh, no. I kept the day job. Or night job. Most of that work was in the dark. Plenty of time to go to school on the side." I could feel her eyes pinned on my profile, could feel her interest in my story. "I was just graduating when D came back a couple of years later with a basic idea to launch a worldwide international ad firm. Recruited me and Nate. Introduced us to his buddy Weston and his almost stepfather-in-law, Dylan—don't ask. It's complicated. The five of us sat down, made a plan together, and here we are. And yes, now I've quit the night work."

"That's crazy admirable." She sounded more impressed than I could have hoped for and also exactly as impressed as I'd always dreamed she'd be.

It *was* pretty impressive when I let myself remember where I'd come from. After I'd run away from Stark, I'd been dirt poor, living on the streets. I hadn't even had my diploma. I'd had to take the GED before college, and now I was co-owner of one of the biggest marketing firms in the world. I burned money just for fun. I wanted for nothing.

Well, that wasn't true.

"I'm not going to pretend I don't like having my ego stroked, but which part specifically was admirable?" I was a total glutton. No denying it. But also, I really wanted to know what she thought. Needed to know.

"All of it," she said. "*All* of it. Changing your look. Working your way up. Becoming somebody. Finding your people. But the part I really admire is the part where someone told you to trust in his vision, and you just...did."

That surprised me, and I was sure that it said something about her that I hadn't realized before. Something big. Another puzzle piece in my hand, but this one I couldn't quite place.

Besides, she was wrong. "Some people would say it was naive."

"But it wasn't naive. Donovan came back with a real plan."

"Some people would call that fool's luck."

She shook her head, adamant. "It wasn't luck. And you're not a fool. You just know how to let yourself believe."

She was still wrong, but I didn't argue. The truth was much more basic, and not impressive in the least. It hadn't mattered whether I believed in Donovan or not.

I just hadn't had anything left to lose.

TWENTY

"Skiing?" Jolie asked as I turned where the highway sign pointed toward Hunter Mountain. "You're taking me skiing? No way. I'm not skiing."

I chuckled as I resumed speed. "Calm your tits. I'm not taking you skiing. I didn't forget you don't know how."

She scowled at me again. "It's been a lot of years. I could have learned."

"But you didn't." It wasn't even a guess. I knew it like I knew anything.

Still, she held out for a beat before admitting I was right. "No, I didn't." Her forehead remained wrinkled in distrust. "You sure as fuck better not be trying to get me to take lessons. And I'm not snowboarding, either."

I tried to imagine that scenario, but it was too absurd to picture. Jolie was one of the strongest women I'd ever met, fearless too, in many ways, but she hated daredevil shit. Heights, fast speeds, anything reckless had always been a hard no. It had taken a lot of convincing just to get her to sneak out to her roof back in the day. I knew what her limits were.

That said, it was possible I was pushing those limits with my plans today. I reassured her all the same. "I'm not signing you up for lessons, and I'm not taking you snowboarding. Chill." As if I wasn't already pressing my luck, I added, "Trust me."

I immediately regretted the words, even as they passed my lips. I definitely deserved her trust, but I didn't like asking for it. I didn't want her to think she could count on me, which was irrational considering how I'd been doing nothing but showing her she could count on me since she walked back into my life.

But it was out there now. The words said, and as though she understood what it cost for me to say them, she answered earnestly. "I do."

She didn't ask again what we were doing at the resort, and we were silent as I found a rather fortunate parking spot near the lodge. Car off, keys in my coat pocket, I gave her my full attention for the first time since we'd started driving. Her expression was wary, but her eyes were bright. She meant it, I realized. That she trusted me. So easily after all this time, when she hadn't trusted me back then.

I didn't know what to make of that or of the way that revelation punched at my gut.

So I didn't try to analyze it. "Let's go."

She followed me without question as we walked up to the lodge and headed for guest services. "Two standard size tubes," I said, pulling out my wallet.

"We're going tubing?" Jolie sounded both intrigued and anxious.

"We'll stick to the kiddie hill. Even three-year-olds can handle it."

"I imagine they're sitting on a parent's lap when they do. They probably also have very little choice in the matter."

I took my card back from the customer rep, pocketed my wallet, then accepted the two passes before turning again to Jolie. "And neither do you it seems." She opened her mouth—to protest, most likely—but I didn't let her. "Here's the receipt so you can pick up our tubes at the counter outside. I'll meet you there in a few."

I left her still gaping and headed to the retail shop before she could argue.

Half of me expected her to follow, but when I chanced a glance over my shoulder a half a minute later, I saw her trudging toward the back doors of the lodge. It felt stupidly good that she would just do what I said without a fight.

Maybe having her trust wasn't so bad after all.

Quickly, I picked out what we needed, not being particular about what I grabbed, and paid for the items, declining a bag. Less than ten minutes later, I found Jolie outside with a blue and a red tube, each awkwardly tucked under an arm.

"Here," I said, throwing a scarf around her neck, then another around mine. I tucked the rest of the clothing into the crook of my arm while I pulled a beanie with the Hunter Mountain logo over her head. It was too intimate, and as my fingers let go of the edge of her hat, I found they were too close to brushing down her cheeks, red from the cold.

"Thank you." Her breath came out in a puff, but it was the color of her tone that was the warmest.

It was that heat that drew me into making another dangerous choice. "You can put those down." I waited while she set the tubes down, each balancing on end between us so they wouldn't be in anyone's way. The barrier between us was good and necessary, but I still resented it as I took one of her hands and put a glove on it like I was a goddamned lady in waiting.

Too close.

Too intimate.

Too fucking dangerous.

Her skin burned against mine as I tugged the waterproof fabric over her fingers. The small gasp she made at the contact told me she felt it too. I zipped the glove on, and without saying anything, she offered her other hand so I could clothe it as well.

Dumb. I was so incredibly dumb.

Especially because this time, I took my time, running the tip of my thumb over the backs of her bare knuckles before presenting the glove. I paused on one digit in particular. "This finger is bare," I said before I could think about it. The thought was a fly I'd tried to keep bottled up, ignoring how it had buzzed inside me, wanting to be free.

With my guard down and the distraction of silky skin, it escaped, and now it buzzed between us.

"It's always been bare."

She didn't belong to anyone. She'd never belonged to anyone.

A weight on my chest lifted, but the fly still buzzed, nagging to know more. "No one's ever tried to put a ring on it?"

"Once." A pause. "Wait. No. Twice."

Twice. Not one but two separate men had thought he was good enough to ask her to be his forever.

"What happened?" I hoped she said that they were both dead. That way I didn't have to go looking for them.

"I had no interest in the one."

Buzz. Buzz. Buzz. "The other?"

She frowned. She'd been solemn, but this was the first time the conversation seemed difficult for her. Her hand turned over so her palm was against mine. "I hurt him very much."

My breath stuck in my lungs. *Me.* She meant me. There was no way she didn't mean me, and acknowledging the past and the pain in that way let loose something in me that was far bigger than a fly. Something more the size of a beast with fangs and predator eyes. A beast that would tear us both apart if I let him.

I stepped back, snatching my palm from hers, and handed her the other glove to put on for herself. Putting on my own gloves and hat, though, I kept thinking about *then*, about the fucked-up proposal I'd made with a pipe cleaner I'd found in my mother's hobby box.

"One day it will be a real ring," I'd promised.

"It doesn't matter. You know I love you."

She'd been crying, and I'd thought for a long time that her tears had been for the situation. For fear of the unknown and where we would go and how it would possibly work out, but every now and then I wondered if they might have been a different kind of tears—the kind shed out of sentimentality and emotion too brimming to keep in.

The way things turned out, that notion seemed unrealistic, but I'd lived long enough to know the complexity of emotions. She could have been crying both kinds of tears all at once. She could have been crying out of happiness and still thrown that happiness away.

But if she hadn't? God, I would have loved her for a lifetime.

It was better not to think about that. Easier too, for both of us I was pretty sure, and when I swatted the fly away and let the topic drop, she didn't try to pick it back up.

The next couple of hours were lost to the stupid thrill of going up and down. The kiddie run was even more tame than I'd imagined, filled with lots of parents and children too young to remember to break for the bathroom without a reminder, yet it was fun all the same. Not much more of a ride than we would have gotten if we'd just gone to Central Park, but I was glad I'd dragged her farther away. The drive had eaten up time and psychologically the distance, made the day feel more like an escape.

She wouldn't talk to me about it, and I'd stopped pressing, but I would have been naive to think that Jolie wasn't carrying a burden at all times, despite the warmth in her eyes and the ease of her smiles. I'd lived a similar past, and I sure as fuck carried shit from those days, so it was a no-brainer that she'd feel the same.

Plus, there was the whole *help-me-kill-my-father* thing. People didn't come to those kinds of decisions without something weighing on them. Point being, she didn't have to say anything for me to know she needed a chance to set down her load and take a vacation from the strain.

Two straight hours of her infectious giggling, and I was confident the day's activity had done the trick.

"One more run?" I asked after we'd taken a break to warm up with hot cocoa in the lodge. We'd been frozen to the bone, despite all the layers, and jonesing to sit by a fire, but after twenty minutes in front of the roaring fireplace, I was thawed enough to go back into the cold.

I watched her as she considered. She'd taken off her gloves, and her scarf was open, revealing the hollow of her neck.

I'd never realized how sexy a throat could be, and I wasn't even thinking about when my cock had been buried inside it.

"Yeah. I could do one more."

I tore my eyes from her neck and took the empty Styrofoam cup from her hand to toss in the recycling along with mine. "One more good run, then we can pick up another round of cocoa for the drive home."

"Sounds perfect."

Outside, we stopped by the counter to get two new tubes, then headed to line up for the conveyor belt that would take us to the top of the hill.

"This was such a great idea," she said as we got in line, and my chest puffed out involuntarily from the praise. "How did you even know about this place?"

"Carla had a boyfriend we lived with for a while in Pough-keepsie. I came here once with some friends from school." I leaned around her to see how many people were in front of us. The crowds had gotten longer as the day had gone on and more skiers abandoned the slopes for tubing. I spied a shorter line next to us, one that led to a longer run. "Here, come this way."

She followed without question. "That's right. I forget that Carla had a life before she remarried."

"I do too." My mother had always been Carla between the two of us. Her days of being Mom had long passed by the time her choices had brought me into Jolie's world. I couldn't hate her for that, no matter what else it had brought me, because knowing Jolie had been the single most gratifying thing in my life. But I'd never forgiven Carla for the rest of it, and these days I rarely thought about her at all.

"I know you haven't talked to her. She's never tried to reach out?"

I glanced behind me at her as I stepped onto the magic carpet, partly to make sure she was still following, but also because of what she'd said. Since she'd been gone for so many years, I'd assumed she didn't have any news from home. "No, she hasn't, thank God. How do you know I haven't talked to her?"

"I went home recently."

She said it all casual, like it was no big deal when instead it was a big fucking clue. "You said you were hiding from your—"

"I was hiding. And then I wasn't."

I adjusted my tube and turned around so I was riding the belt facing backward. I had so many questions but was very aware that she would have told me already if this was stuff she wanted me to know.

But she was talking now. So did that mean she was ready to answer?

"He found you." Guessing felt more sure than questioning, but it still felt tentative. Like I was walking out onto a frozen pond, trying to decide how long the ice would hold.

She gazed in the distance to where the sun was starting to get low in the sky. "No."

"Something he did drew you out."

She avoided the question-not-question. "I didn't lie when I said I didn't know anything current about him. I wasn't home long enough to learn anything useful."

Asking what happened with Langdon was useless. I blew out a breath that steamed in the air like the exhale from a cigarette. "But you were home long enough to figure out I haven't talked to Carla?"

She gave a cute shrug, her lips puckering as she did. "I might have asked about you while I was there."

"What else do you know about me?"

"Hmm." Her cheeks went rosy. Probably from the cold and not the conversation. "I know you've never had a ring on your finger either."

"They know that much about my life?" I'd thought I'd gone as dark from the people back home as they'd gone for me.

"No, actually, that..." Now she definitely blushed. "I Googled. Public record says Cade Warren has always been single."

We were still moving, but I swore the earth stood still. I'd known she had to look me up in order to email me to meet with her. That didn't require looking at public records. She'd looked that up because she'd wanted to know.

Why had she wanted to know?

Why did it mean so much that she did?

My feet hit snow as the belt came to an end. Since I hadn't been watching, I hadn't been expecting it, and Jolie crashed into me. I put my arms out to steady her. To steady us. She shivered as my free hand found her waist, and after I stepped us to the side and out of the way, I left them there. She took a step in, bringing us even closer, despite the tubes we carried, and for a second I thought we were having a moment.

Then she realized we weren't at the top of the kiddie run.

"Hold on a minute." She walked out of my grasp, scanning the hill in front of us and the belt we'd just come up, obviously realizing she'd been tricked. "No way. Not a chance. I'm not going down that."

"You've been fine all day. Why suddenly get cold feet?"

"Because this run is twice as long!"

"Three times as long, I think." I wasn't helping myself. "Which means you have three times the fun."

"I don't think it works like that."

"It works exactly like that. Longer run just means extending the thrill."

"I was happy with the length of thrill before." She gave a tight smile to someone behind me. "Go ahead! We're not going down."

"Yes, actually, we are, but please go before us. We need a second."

The teens behind us grinned as they stepped around us, a blunt contrast to the glare Jolie gave me. "I'm not going down that hill, Cade. You can do whatever you want, but I'm not going down."

"I have news for you, sweetheart. There's not another way down."

She spun around to see if I was telling the truth, which I might not have been. It was possible there was a pathway that could be walked, but it wasn't obvious if there was.

Realizing that she'd have to ask, she stepped toward the attendant at the top of the run. "Excuse me?"

The kid—he couldn't have been more than twenty-five—answered with what he presumed Jolie wanted to know. "Sitting in the tube is all that's allowed. No belly rides. You can get in place here, and I'll get you started down the hill."

While he'd given his rote delivery, I'd taken the opportunity to pull a hundred out of my wallet and slapped it in his palm before Jolie could correct him with her real question. "Take care of this, will you?" I handed him my tube and took Jolie's from her.

She relaxed, assuming I was helping her find another way

down the mountain, but instead of handing the man her tube as well, I plopped it on the ground and sat down, pulling Jolie in my lap. "Don't struggle if you want this to stay safe, and hold on tight."

"What are you—?"

I pushed off, sending the tube down the mountain, and her question turned into a high-pitched squeal.

"No lap riders over forty-four inches tall!" The attendant called after us, too late.

Seriously, what did he think the hundred had been for? Like I'd pay that much for him just to return my tube for me.

Whatever he thought, he'd lost his chance to stop us. We were tearing down the run at full speed, the wind whipping, Jolie screaming and laughing and screaming again. She clung onto the handles, and I clung onto her and tried to ignore her ass in my lap, and the way it rubbed against my cock whenever the tube took a little bit of a jump. I hadn't quite expected how bumpy the ride would be. Turned out the difference between the kiddie runs and the regular runs really was more than just length.

But God, it was fucking thrilling.

Because it was always thrilling to soar at a wicked speed through space, but we could have been sitting still, and I would have been just as thrilled because she was in my arms, and she was happy, and once upon a time that right there had been The Dream.

I wished the ride could have gone on forever.

At the bottom, after we scurried to our feet and rushed our tube out of the way as was protocol, I expected her to attack. A snowball in the face, maybe. At least a good tongue-lashing, even though she'd obviously had a good time and had most likely felt the evidence of my good time as I'd grown thick and hard beneath her.

Instead, when she'd caught her breath, her eyes were still gleaming and her smile still pasted to her face. My hands were still around her, too. Or around her again, and the way she kept looking at my lips, I wondered if maybe she was thinking about kissing me.

That might have been a real punishment.

Just thinking about it stole my own smile from my face. She sombered when I did, and then it felt even more likely that we might kiss.

I didn't think I could survive that.

It had been one thing to have her mouth wrapped around my cock. Her lips on mine was a whole other level of connection. One that would surely kill me.

And despite the danger, I couldn't fucking step away. "See?" I said, desperate for something safe to fill the silence. "Not so scary when it's both of us together."

She grew even more serious. "I forgot that. That I'm stronger with you."

"I didn't." Fuck. This wasn't safe at all.

"No, you always knew. I wish I'd thought that would have been enough."

Her regrets meant nothing.

Maybe that wasn't true. "I've been mad at you for a really long time because you didn't believe in us, Jol."

"And now?" It was a whisper, as though the question might break something if voiced too loudly. "Are you still mad?"

Fuck, yes, I was mad. Mad was all I ever was. It had been the only emotion I'd truly known for so long now that I didn't remember what it felt like not to be mad.

Except, all of a sudden, that wasn't true either. "I want to be," I said, and I was bare and naked now before her.

"But you're not?"

Everything about her was hopeful. Her expression, the way she held her body, the soft lilt in her voice. It was the perfect chance to say something hurtful to her, to get back for how hurt she'd once made me when I'd been full of hope and looking at her with the same trusting eyes.

Revenge had been a nice fantasy over the years. I'd conjured up many scenarios where I'd given paybacks. Both to her father and her. The times I'd dreamed about destroying her had been the most satisfying.

Right now, I couldn't imagine why I'd ever want to hurt her. Hurting her only meant hurting me, and hadn't I been hurt enough?

So where did that leave me emotionally? "I don't think I'm ready for what I feel."

She nodded. "I don't think I'm ready either."

Then, because she'd said she wasn't ready—because caring for her and protecting her was what I always did, what I'd always done—I stepped away, without kissing her, without even a last lingering glance at her mouth.

But if she thought I'd stepped away because I was protecting myself? Well. I kind of hoped that's exactly what she thought.

TWENTY-ONE

P *ast*

I FLATTENED myself against the roof and bent over the over-hang, checking to make sure the window was slightly open before I knocked. That was our code—if the window was shut, it was a bad time. That way I didn't pop up when her father might see me. We'd become masters at secrecy. It was funny what skills necessity could instill.

Almost as soon as I rapped, as though she'd been waiting for me, her curtains parted, and Jolie lifted her window all the way. Carefully, I turned around and lowered my foot to the open ledge, then worked my way through the opening onto her bed, where she immediately threw her arms around me.

"I swear I can't breathe every time you do that."

I knew she was looking behind me, at the drop from the second floor to the ground. The height was even worse here than around the front of the house because the basement opened up to garden level on this side. No sane person would attempt to get to Jolie this way, which was probably why Headmaster Stark had put her in this room.

Headmaster Stark hadn't been counting on me.

"I could climb it in my sleep," I insisted. But I tore myself away from her and shut the windowpane because keeping it open felt like tempting fate.

I started to pull her back to my arms when she reminded me. "The dresser."

Stark was the kind of guy who locked his daughter in her room at night. Literally. The threat of her having no way out in a fire was apparently less frightening than the threat of her sneaking out. The high window took care of one possible route of escape—or so he thought. A lock on the outside of her door took care of the other route.

If he wanted to walk into her room, the only warning we'd get would be the click of the lock turning, and while both of us agreed it was highly unlikely he'd come to check on her in the middle of the night, Jolie insisted on taking precautions all the same.

And so her dresser was pushed in front of the door. It wasn't heavy enough to keep anyone out for long, but it could buy me time to go back through the window.

"One day, he's going to come up here because he hears us sliding the dresser against the door." I tugged it into place all the same while she pushed with her shoulder on the other side.

"It makes me feel better." It was what she always said, and I understood that too, but it was the same reason that made her feel better that made me hate the safeguard—I was the one who was protected. Not her.

But that was the price of her love. She looked out for me, and when it came to avoiding the wrath of her father, she was the expert. And as I moved with her back to the bed, I promised myself, as I always did, that one day I would be the one who did all the protecting.

Back in her arms, my lips found hers, teasing them open with soft kisses before claiming her with my tongue. I was at turns aggressive and gentle, a technique I'd only recently realized drove her wild—the chase, the retreat, the chase again. That was exactly how Jolie wanted to be pursued. She wanted to be wanted but couldn't handle being wanted all at the same time, and the push/pull seemed to allow her space to process both feelings separately.

Driving her wild, though, meant I'd just set the agenda for our tryst. I'd wanted to talk to her first. Truth was, I missed her. We'd been avoiding each other publicly the past couple of weeks, sure her father was onto us, a fear that could very well have been imagined. Regardless, we'd been playing it safe, and while I loved the physical with her—love wasn't even the right term; I craved it, needed it, depended on it for my survival—our connection went beyond that. I yearned to know every part of her, to be the keeper of her every secret, both the important ones and the trivial. My heart beat more steadily in her presence. Keeping my distance had been agony, and I wanted to catch up. There was the thing I wanted to ask her too, the pipe cleaner from my mother's craft kit burning like a hot coal in my pocket.

But I also wanted this—her panting and eager, her mouth everywhere, her hands tugging at my sweatshirt.

I broke away long enough to get the thing over my head. By the time I'd tossed it to the ground, she was already climbing onto me, straddling my lap, grinding her hips against the aching rod in my jeans.

With a grunt of satisfaction, I unthinkingly leaned back and jerked at the unexpected surge of pain as my body met the decorative framework around the window.

Jolie, of course, noticed. "Is it still really bad? Does it need more ointment? I'm pretty sure I could get an antibiotic if I faked a sore throat."

"Carla had something from her last toothache that she never finished. I stole those." Carefully, I repositioned myself so I was leaning against the flat of the wall instead of the uneven molding. "It's healing pretty well, I think."

It had been worse this time than usual. He'd brought out a cane instead of his skinny-tailed whip, and the single stripe he'd left had torn open and bled. It had been more than a week since I'd slept on my back, and only the last few days that I'd been able to go long stretches without thinking about it at all.

I downplayed the pain for her, though. Partly because it had been her father who'd made it, and I didn't want her to feel any guilt about that.

But also because I was ashamed of it. Ashamed that I'd been stupid enough to get myself in trouble. Ashamed of what had happened in that room after the cane had broken my skin.

I still hadn't told her all of it. She carried enough on her own. I didn't need her to feel this pain with me too.

"Turn around. Let me see it."

I shook my head and tried to pull her back toward me. The heat of the moment was ruined now, but if I let her examine me, she'd turn into my nurse, and I didn't need that kind of attention right now.

She resisted for a moment, then sighed and stretched out,

her legs tangling with mine, her head resting on my chest. "How long do we have to hold on?"

"It's only two months. Less, actually. Seven weeks." I pressed my lips against her forehead and stroked her hair. "We just have to get through seven weeks, and then we're gone."

"Tell me again how we're going to do it."

This was becoming as routine as the window being left open and the dresser pulled in front of the door, me reciting how we'd eventually get away like it was her favorite bedtime story. "We'll walk the stage. We'll get our diplomas. Then after the ceremony, we'll leave. We won't even go to the after party. We'll just be gone."

"And we won't take his car."

"No. We won't take my mother's either."

"So they can't come after us saying we stole anything." This was one of the most important details to her, the part she went over and over. She rarely expressed fear where her father was concerned—because she'd learned to keep it buried, I suspected. Her hyperfocus on making sure there was no legal way her father could come after us revealed the terror she usually kept hidden.

"We won't take anything of theirs," I promised. "And you'll be eighteen then. He can't call you a runaway." Her birthday was only three days before graduation. I'd already had mine. Both of us would be adults in the eyes of the law.

"And you're sure Janice won't press charges about her truck?"

"Yes." I wasn't as sure as I pretended I was, but I felt good enough to count on it. Janice was the school's gardener. These days, she did more delegating than actual work, but she still occupied the cottage attached to the greenhouse on the edge of the school property. The truck we planned to take had belonged to her late husband and had sat unused in her garage since his death the previous year.

I'd heard all about it when I'd been sentenced to weed pulling for one of my punishments. Official punishment, anyway. The one that had been declared to my fellow school-mates as a warning to not get caught with a joint. My real punishment had been doled out in the privacy of Stark's office, the door closed, my mouth biting down into my shirt so that I wouldn't be heard down the hall. Any sound at all would equal double the thrashing, so I tried extra hard to be quiet. I hadn't learned as well as Jolie had, but I'd learned some.

The greenhouse part of the punishment had ended up being more of a reward. Mostly I moved heavy bags of soil and dug holes, but it was calm and meditative, the hours filled with a gentle rhythm of work as Janice chatted about her husband and her refusal to learn to drive a stick and the truck that still worked but she hadn't gotten around to selling. More than once she said that I could buy it from her, and when I told her that I didn't have the money, she'd always say, "We'll figure some-thing out." She'd even shown me where the keys were kept.

We could take the truck, I'd decided. We could write a note explaining. She wouldn't report us. I hoped.

"We'll send her money when we can," Jolie said, repeating the promise I'd made in the past.

"We will. We'll be fine."

"And where will we go?"

This was where the story changed from telling to telling. Sometimes I'd say we'd go to New York. Other times, Canada. On days when one of us was feeling especially pessimistic, I'd take us farther—to Europe. To Egypt. To Japan.

Truth was, where we went didn't matter. As long as I was with her.

I tipped her chin up toward mine so I could look her in the eyes when I said it. But then her mouth caught my attention as she swept her tongue over her bottom lip, and the hand she'd been lazily dancing over my abdomen suddenly felt like not enough touch.

I pressed my mouth to hers, pulling her leg astride me so that my cock could press against the warm spot between her legs. "I need to be inside of you," I whispered between drugging kisses. "That's the only place I want to go."

Sex was Jolie's love language even more than it was mine, and that was all I had to say before she was stripping off her girly nightie and scrambling out of her cotton panties. I toed off my shoes and stripped off my jeans. Digging for the condom in my pocket before I tossed them aside, my fingers brushed against the pipe cleaner, and I considered briefly if now was the time for my proposal.

But then she was naked, the moonlight streaming through the window like a spotlight on her beauty, and my cock turned so hard that it became the priority. I tore open the wrapper with my teeth, slid on the latex, and pushed her down to the bed.

She spread her legs to make room for me, and I climbed between and hovered over her, my weight balanced on my palm placed on the bed next to her head.

"Are you ready for me?" My free hand was checking even as I asked, slipping between her folds to find her wet and slick. She hadn't been the first girl I'd ever fucked—I hadn't been her first either—but she'd been the first girl I'd fucked long enough to actually feel like I knew what I was doing.

I had a pretty good feeling I was the first person who'd made it good for her, and that was worth more than being the only person who'd ever been inside her. I prided myself on making sure I always made it good for her, hoping that would keep me special, and so after finding her wet, I dragged my fingers up to swirl against her swollen bud.

"Are *you* ready for *me*?" she teased, her back arching as I hit an especially sensitive spot.

I was always ready for her.

And I never was.

It was a paradox. How those things could exist together and be true was beyond the capability of my teenage mind, but the reality of it sent a shiver of apprehension down my spine even as I rushed to get myself inside of her.

We were still clumsy at this part—one of us usually needing to use a hand to get my head notched up to the right place—and this time I was still in the process of lining up when she lifted her hips and pulled me inside her.

I shuddered at the sudden damp heat as I buried myself to my balls.

No, I was never ready for her.

But I was ready to be hers. For always. Ready for her to be mine. With each thrust, I felt more and more like we already belonged to each other, like each push into her was me giving her another piece of myself, and each pull out was me taking another piece of her.

And so what if I was only eighteen and sentimental? Some things deserved to be romanticized. Some moments deserved to be treasured. Some bonds deserved to be glorified and worshipped like the unbreakable covenant of a God to his people. That was the kind of connection we had. Fucking her was holy. The only communion I'd ever believed in. Sex, a sacred act that made us one.

"I love you." She brought her hands to my face and kissed me between breaths. "I love you so much."

Then I was coming, before I could say it back, before I could spend the time needed to make her come too, before I could register the rattle of the knob and the door knocking against the dresser.

"What the hell is this, Julianna?" Stark's voice hissed through the open crack.

We jumped apart. Scrambled like the breaking in a game of pool. I got my jeans on without removing the condom. My shoes, I grabbed without bothering to put on.

Meanwhile, Jolie opened the window and started looking for my shirt. "Where is it? *Where is it?*" Her whisper felt like a yell.

The dresser was moving. Slowly, but surely. Stark was putting his back into his push, cursing and demanding that Julianna *open the door right this instance.*

We didn't have any time.

"If you find it, stuff it under the bed." I was already sitting on the windowsill. I had to pull myself out, then crouch, placing my feet flat on the sill so I could reach up and hoist myself the way I came. Normally, I took my time climbing out. If I did it too fast and didn't have a firm grip on the overhang above me, I would fall to the ground below.

I glanced down.

I'd survive it. It would probably hurt, but I'd definitely survive.

I wasn't sure that would be the case if I stayed.

Jolie knelt on the bed, her face etched with terror, her eyes wide. "Be careful." She glanced to the door and back at me. "Be careful, but go!"

I hesitated, just long enough to give her a reassuring nod. I was going to be okay. She was going to be okay. She'd already had the foresight to make up a story about why she'd moved the dresser—*she'd heard a noise. She was scared.* Her father wouldn't know there was a boy creeping on the roof above them as she explained.

The hesitation was where I'd gone wrong—that damned desire to make sure she was okay, even when the best way to make her okay was to be gone. It was instinctive and my weakness.

In that half second of time, Stark got the door open and saw me hanging out the window without a shirt on, saw his daughter naked and trying to help get me out.

I'd thought I'd seen the man in all states of anger, thought I'd seen the worst of his wrath, but the look on his face expressed a whole new level of rage. "You're dead, Cade Warren."

Even without the venom in his tone, I knew he meant what he said. He'd shown himself to be quite reliable when it came to follow-through on his threats.

With no time and no choice, I had no chance of climbing up.

I didn't let myself think.

I grabbed onto the bottom of the window, swung my legs out, and dropped to the ground.

TWENTY-TWO

P *resent*

WE SPENT the next two days avoiding each other.

I didn't know what was going on in her head, but I knew what was going on in mine, and what was going on was complicated. For the first time in years, I verged on optimism, and that felt dangerous and fragile. I'd gotten used to the idea that I'd always be alone. The possibility that I might have someone—that I could have *her*—thrilled me, but I didn't know how to let that notion sit in my head. My muscles literally tensed against it. As if they remembered the physical pain that came with feeling things for Julianna Stark.

My heart was a whole other sort of tense. I'd developed a constant ache in the center of my chest. It hurt to breathe, and both Tuesday and Wednesday nights, when I lay in the dark straining my ears to hear any sound from her in the next room, my lungs struggled to work altogether. Each intake stuttered as I fought to bring air in. Each exhale went so long I felt completely empty before I was able to attempt another draw.

I tried not to wonder if Jolie was going through something similar.

At the same time, I didn't believe she had the right to anguish. She'd been the one to desert me. What did she have to fear about reconnecting? What did she stand to lose that she hadn't willingly given up?

Whatever she was grappling with, it made her skittish and quiet. She left the hotel room for long stretches of time without saying a word about where she was going or when she'd be back. Not like I told her where I was going when I disappeared to go to the gym or the office or the hotel bar. I told myself I didn't care, but twice I found myself following her at a discreet distance. Once she ended up at the Midtown Library. The other time she slipped into a church. Both times I'd lingered outside in the cold, smoking from a pack of Camels that I'd finally broken down and purchased. Both times I psyched myself up, saying as soon as I got to the butt, I'd go in after her. I'd confront her with every tangled-up emotion. I'd force her to hear everything I had to say.

Both times, my will dissolved when the cigarette had turned to ash. I stomped out the cherry and left her for my own distractions.

By Thursday afternoon, the hotel suite had become a living hell.

I'd spent most of the day locked in my bedroom and tried to catch up on what was going on in the Tokyo office. Besides the fact that I couldn't concentrate, everyone on the other side of the world was asleep or trying to be, and after the third time I woke my assistant up to ask her a question that I should have been able to figure out on my own, I decided to give up on the attempt.

I shut my laptop and looked at the clock. A quarter past four. The hours were ticking down until Jolie left. With Donovan on board to help with her father, there wasn't any need for me to stay involved. She'd get on that plane, and we could go back to being strangers.

Was it too early to start drinking?

Close enough. The numb side effect of alcohol lured me to venture out of my room to the minibar. When I came out, she was on her bed, wearing nothing but my goddamn T-shirt and her panties, painting her toenails bright red. She glanced at me quickly before going back to her task.

Fuck, even that had memories attached. All the times she'd pull out a brightly colored bottle and decorate her toes, only to wipe them clean with acetone when she was finished since her father didn't approve.

One day, I'll always have painted toes.

I popped off the lid on a beer bottle and chugged a quarter of it down right there. I would have drunk more if my cell phone hadn't started ringing.

"What have you got?" I said when I saw it was Donovan.

Jolie returned her attention to me, either because she was nosy or because she suspected the call might be in regard to her. I turned my body so I wasn't looking at her, but I could feel her eyes boring into me all the same.

"I'd rather discuss it in the office." Donovan's tone refused any argument, which was a sure-fire way to make me combative.

"I can discuss things perfectly fine on the phone."

"I'm sure you can, asshole, but this isn't the kind of information that should be shared over unsecured lines. And the information isn't complete yet. I need you to run an errand first."

I muttered a curse under my breath. "Fine. I'll be there in a bit."

"I'm coming with," Jolie said as soon as I'd hung up.

I ran my hand over my beard and took another pull on the bottle, trying to decide if I should fight her on it. If it was about her quest, then she should probably be allowed to be there. But I'd spent the last two days trying not to be with her.

Being with her was also exactly what I wanted most.

As I shifted toward her, her eyes caught mine, and the decision was made. "We're leaving in twenty."

"Awesome." It was the first time I'd seen her smile since Hunter Mountain, and I suddenly couldn't remember how I ever existed without it. "Good thing that was the second coat."

I drank my beer and watched as she capped the polish, then walked carefully down the hallway. A few seconds later, I heard the hair dryer go on. Drying her wet nails, I suspected.

It almost had *me* smiling.

The impulse disappeared when my phone dinged with a text from Donovan. **Come looking mean.**

The skin at the back of my neck prickled. *Look mean* was code for *I need you to do something shady with some even shadier people.* I'd handled a few of these kinds of interactions for Donovan before. The man might have a dangerous brain, but I doubted he could throw a punch to save his life. He certainly didn't look like a threat.

My size was threatening on its own. Add the tats and my perma-scowl, and I could look very intimidating. It helped that I was rough around the edges, no matter how well I was dressed. In fact, while I'd spent my earlier days of thug life in black jeans and black T-shirts, I'd since found I was more menacing in a suit. Good thing I still had a clean one hanging in the closet.

But now I had a problem. Whatever Donovan needed me to do, I wasn't going to want Jolie with me.

I started down the hallway to tell her and stopped halfway there. Telling her she couldn't come would mean taking away that smile. A few days ago, I would have done it willingly. On purpose. Because I wanted her to feel as bad as I did every day.

When exactly had I stopped wanting that?

She could at least come hear what Donovan had dug up so far. No harm in that.

"MISSING TEENS?" Jolie looked to me, even though it had been Donovan who had delivered the information.

I hadn't told her about the pattern of runaways that he'd mentioned on Tuesday, not only because that would have required a conversation when I'd been avoiding her, but because it hadn't seemed like anything real yet.

Apparently, now it was.

"Thirteen in all. Fourteen if you count Cade, which I'm not. It wouldn't be notable if any of them had shown up again. As it is, there are thirteen teenagers who were last seen at Stark Academy and never again." He spoke in a hushed tone. It had been after five when we'd arrived, but Donovan had set the glass to the opaque setting and shut the door as soon as we had. The conversation was obviously one he didn't want overheard.

Understandably so. Since there was a real good chance we were talking about thirteen kids who were very likely dead.

"And you think my father has something to do with that?" Again she looked to me, as if I could somehow translate whatever it was that she was having trouble understanding.

Donovan gave a slight shake of his head. "Not necessarily. But if he isn't responsible, it's an opportunity to blame him."

This time I was the one who looked at her. I watched the color slowly drain from her face as she processed what he was proposing. It was one thing to destroy her father for the things he'd actually done. It was another to frame him for murder.

Personally, I didn't have a problem with it.

Jolie seemed to need to sit with it a minute.

"We don't have to decide what we do until we have more info," Donovan said in an attempt to soothe her. "We might get lucky and discover your father's responsible for all of it."

So much for putting her at ease.

"I'm sure your dad didn't...*hurt* them." I wasn't really sure of that, but I couldn't bring myself to say the words *murder* or *kill* or any other synonyms.

I actually wasn't sure he hadn't taken their lives. While I didn't think he was a secret serial killer, he had predispositions. He was a sadist. He liked to inflict pain. He got off on the sight of blood.

"On purpose, anyway," I amended. I could totally see a punishment gone too far kind of scenario.

But thirteen times?

Her skeptical glare said it was pointless to try to sell her a lie. She knew who her father was as well as I did. "You're sure they totally disappeared? Maybe they just changed their names. Didn't want to be found again. I know, thirteen kids is a lot, but it's not impossible."

"It's not," Donovan agreed. "I had my guy try to trace them down. Honestly, I expected it to take a while. This isn't the kind of investigation work that happens overnight, and if he were searching any of these kids individually, he probably wouldn't have found anything yet. But looking for them as a bunch, he stumbled upon something useful."

"That sounds ominous." I was beginning to regret having brought Jolie. As much as she wanted her father gone, I wasn't sure she wanted to know he'd been as much of a monster as Donovan was suggesting.

"My guy's contact says he has definitive proof of what happened to those kids. That's all I know. That's all he'll say until he's paid." He reached under the desk, brought out a black briefcase, and set it in front of him. He entered a code, and the case popped open, revealing stacks of money. "The contact has the code as well. He and I are the only ones able to open the case. He'll take the money, replace it with the proof we're looking for, then he'll lock the case again. Bring it back to me, and we'll go over it together."

Jolie's eyes were wide at the sight of the cash. "You're paying that much for this information?"

The money wasn't what had me bugged. I could pay him back without blinking. "We're the ones who want it. Why's he need to lock it?"

"Because I'm not just paying for info for you. He's handing over something for me as well. Which is why I have no problem paying the money."

In other words, it wasn't any of my business.

He'd been looking directly at Jolie. Now he stared at me. "The info is free of charge. As long as you do the collecting."

"Got it." My pulse had already ticked up with adrenaline the way it did before I stepped into a ring to spar. I enjoyed being behind a desk, managing people. Making legit money. But there was a part of me that felt more suited to being a heavy. A year spent as Stark's punching bag had given me a desire to possess the power of being on the other side, and while I didn't feel the need to pursue that full-time, I did love the thrill now and then.

Donovan shut the briefcase and reentered the code before handing it over to me. "Good. The meeting's set for six."

I checked my watch. "Cutting it close, aren't we?"

"Meetup is six blocks away. You can walk it in ten."

Jolie stood up before I did. "We should go now. Get there early."

Before I got the chance to correct her, Donovan did it for me. "Not you, kid. This is a job just for Cade."

The kid remark likely ruffled her as much as being told no. Especially since Jolie was a couple of years older than Donovan. Grateful as I was that I didn't have to be the one to ban her from the trip, I kind of wanted to punch him in the dick for patronizing her.

But Jolie could stick up for herself. "I'm not a kid, thank you very much, and I'm the one who is destroying my father, not Cade. He's *helping* me. Which means I go with him, and that's that."

Donovan glared at me, a look that could only mean *would you set the woman straight?*

I was of half a mind to let him work it out himself, but I knew how nasty he could get when he wanted to win, and I didn't have any intention of letting Jolie come. "He's right. This is just me."

"That's ridiculous. I don't want you doing me—" She cut herself off. "Hold on. Are you implying that this is dangerous?"

I'd thought that had been obvious. "That's exactly what I'm implying."

At the same time, Donovan said, "Not at all. Just very unnecessary."

His response was admittedly better. Gave her less to worry about.

"Right. What he said. It's cold out. I'll be in and out. Stay here, stay warm, and we'll open it up when I get back. I won't have anything before you do."

She wasn't fooled. "If it's dangerous, even more reason for me to go. This is *my* thing, Cade. I know you said for you, not for me, but fuck that. I came to you. I'm not asking you to go into a dangerous situation on my behalf."

Donovan stood up to meet her at that level. "Look. I know you're trying to watch out for him, but he can take care of himself. Trust me."

Sure seemed like it too, with him defending me.

I stood to gain some power. "You didn't ask me. I'm choosing."

"I'm not *letting* you." Her eyes were pleading, her jaw set, and as much as I wasn't going to tolerate some woman telling me what I could and couldn't do, I did feel a tightness in my chest over her concern.

"You're not going, Jolie. Get that through your head now, or I won't share the information I get."

"You're destroying him without me now?"

"Sure. Why not? Like I said—like you reminded me—I'm not doing this for you." My eye twitched from the lie.

Which was weird because when had it stopped being the truth?

Fortunately, she couldn't read me that well anymore, and after a beat, her expression went hard. "Fuck you both very much." She grabbed her coat off the back of the chair. "I'm not waiting here for you while you traipse around the underworld, probably getting yourself killed. And I'm not spending another minute with *him*." She glared at Donovan. I would have been much happier about her being upset with him if she wasn't also upset with me. "I'll be waiting in the lobby." She stormed out the door, letting it slam behind her.

I'd started after her, without thinking, when he stopped me. "Let her go. She's upset, but she's safe. This is definitely not a meeting you want her attending."

It took a couple of deep breaths before I turned back toward him. "This guy's that scary?"

"Not sure. It's my first dealing with him. My contact vouches for him, but he also emphasized caution. The amount of money being exchanged and what I'm getting in return is enough reason to be wary." He moved to the bookcase while he spoke, where his safe was hidden behind a fake shelf. He opened it up and removed a loaded semi-automatic handgun. "Here's this, just in case."

I put my coat on before taking it, sticking it into the inside pocket that I'd had made specifically for hiding a gun. It had been a while since I'd carried one. The weight against my chest felt both exhilarating and foreboding. The thrill of danger was a nice perk of running Donovan's dirty errands. The actuality of it was the downside.

I was suddenly curious about what I'd be transporting. "What is it I'm bringing back to you?"

He waved his hand dismissively. "Nothing that interesting. It's the info you're getting about the kids that's valuable. Didn't want to worry your girl, but it took some heavy negotiating to even get the conversation started. Someone really doesn't want this information out."

He was feeding me some bullshit somewhere. Either he really didn't want me knowing what he was involved with or what he'd discovered about the missing teens was a whole lot bigger than Stark.

I knew him well enough to know he wouldn't tell me any more easily, and with twenty minutes left to six, I didn't have time to push. "Where am I meeting up with this guy?"

He gave me the info, along with a shot of whiskey. Liquor was always a good idea before these errands. Not too much to cloud the head, but enough to steady the nerves.

"Call me after. I can meet you at the hotel, if that's easier. I know you'll want Jolie with you when we open the case up. You know she's going to try to get you to let her come with you, right?"

I'd already considered that. "I'll put her in the cab myself." I straightened my collar, rechecked the gun, buttoned my coat, picked up the briefcase. "Oh, and Donovan? She's not my girl."

He threw out some rebuttal, but I'd already left.

And truthfully, I was having trouble finding the will to deny it.

TWENTY-THREE

"I'm going with you," Jolie said as soon as I found her in the lobby downstairs.

Sometimes I fucking hated it when Donovan was right.

Without saying anything, I ushered her out the main doors, pretending it didn't feel natural to touch the small of her back.

Outside, I dropped my hand and walked to the edge of the sidewalk so I could signal a cab.

She trotted after, pleading her case the whole time. "I'll be quiet. I won't interfere. I can stay outside if you really want me to. I won't be in the way. I just need to go with you."

Miracle of miracles, a taxi pulled over toward us immediately. I didn't speak until it was at the curb, and I had the door opened for her. "Where you need to go is back to the hotel."

She didn't move, her hands clenched into fists at her sides. "You can't keep me from going with you. I want to go. Why can't I go?"

"Why do you want to come?" I sounded tired and frustrated because I was. I needed to be getting my head in the right place, and she was distracting me, pulling my focus, throwing me off my game.

"He's my blood relative, not yours. I should take the responsibility of his sins."

"You took responsibility. You asked me for my help. So let me do the thing I'm good at, and wait for me at the hotel so we can go over what I come back with together."

"And if it's dangerous, you shouldn't go alone. You should have backup. You could get hurt. "

Like she could protect me.

But what I said was worse. "Since when do you care what happens to me?"

She retracted as though I'd slapped her, her eyes glistening. "Is that what you think? You think I don't care?"

The cab driver honked his horn, but I ignored him. "Have you given me any reason to think otherwise?"

She blinked several times, and her jaw got tight, her mouth a straight line. "I guess that's how you'd see it."

Damn straight. Because I wasn't an idiot. Because I'd been there.

"Hey, lady. You getting in or not?" The driver had his head cranked over his shoulder, waiting for Jolie's answer.

"She's getting in." This time when I pushed at her, she got in and hugged her arms over her chest, refusing to look at me.

Well, that was fine. She could be mad. Like Donovan said, she'd also be safe.

"She's staying at the Park Hyatt." I reached over her to hand the driver some bills. "This should cover the cost."

I hesitated for a moment before closing the door, wanting to say something, not sure what that something was.

After a beat, I figured it was best to let things lie. I shut the door and hit the roof of the cab, letting the driver know he could take off.

I was tempted to watch after her, but I knew that would be a mistake. Turning away from the street, I set down the briefcase, pulled a Camel from my pocket, and lit it. The rhythmic act of smoking was a great way to get focused. I needed to be on my toes. Needed to be completely in the moment.

Needed to stop thinking about what she'd meant when she said, *I guess that's how you'd see it.*

Why would I see it any other way? Had I missed something? Was she saying she *did* care?

It was a detail I could run away with, if I let myself.

I couldn't let myself.

Shaking my head of all Jolie thoughts, I took a long drag of my smoke, picked up the case, and set off toward my destination.

THE MEETING POINT was at the edge of Midtown, right where it met up with Hell's Kitchen. Admittedly, the area had a bit of grit, but the luxury apartment building across the street made it an unsuspecting location for dirty deals.

Truth was, the more upscale meetup spots were the ones that put me most on guard. Upscale meant money, and people with money were, in my experience, the most dangerous.

I slipped into the alleyway between a grocery store and a restaurant that served Cuban cuisine and counted doors until I came to the fifth one. My watch said it was a minute to six. Right on time.

I knocked.

A burly man in a black suit opened the door. He didn't make eye contact, scanning both directions in the alley behind me instead. "Entrance to the restaurant is round front. We don't take deliveries after five."

I responded with what I'd been instructed to say. "I'm here for Bishop."

With a nod of his head, Burly Man pushed the door open, his jacket lifting so I could see the glock he was packing. "Upstairs. You'll know the room."

I resisted the urge to pat my gun. It was a typical interaction for this sort of thing, and my spidey senses didn't detect anything out of the ordinary, but there was a reason I'd moved out of dirty work. Even typical interactions had the likelihood of going bad.

Cautiously, I stepped past him, scanning the room as he'd scanned the street. It was a typical back-of-restaurant loading area. I could hear the scrape of pots and pans from the kitchen just ahead, and beyond that, as a swinging door flew open, the buzz of New Yorkers hoping to finish their meal in time to catch a show.

The staircase ran to my left—a standard narrow corridor that practically gave a person claustrophobia to climb through. Of course the light was out, and the stairs were steep, and the briefcase bumped against the wall with each step, but I was at the top soon enough. There I found a dark hallway, the only light coming from a room at the end.

Aren't you supposed to not go toward the light?

I chuckled at the thought as I walked the hall, careful to make noise so I wouldn't surprise anyone. I stopped at the threshold, thrown a little off guard by the sight of five overtly armed men stationed around the room. A bigwig sat behind a desk at the far side. A skinny lackey type perched on the edge as though they'd been consulting on some matter.

All eyes were on me.

Now this was a little atypical. Usually these deals were conducted with even teams.

I reassured myself that Donovan knew what he was doing—fuck, he better know what he was doing—and addressed the bigwig. "You Bishop?"

It was the man I'd thought was the lackey who answered. "I'm Bishop. You Beasley's guy?"

"That I am." Beasley was the name Donovan used when he did shady deals.

Bishop, which was likely a pseudonym as well, gestured toward the briefcase in my hand. "That for me?"

"You have something for me in exchange?"

He worked his mouth like he had snuff tucked in his lip and ignored the question. "Put her here."

I paused. I preferred not to hand over money without seeing the goods first, but I wasn't sure I was in a position to have demands. I swept my gaze around the room, noting that though none of the heavies had a weapon drawn, they were each at the ready. It was a lot of protection for a simple exchange. What the fuck had Stark gotten mixed up with?

Or was it the information Donovan was seeking that was so valuable?

Either way, I needed to be cautious. "Seems I'm at a clear disadvantage here. I'm expected to hand this over with no promise I'll get what I'm after in return?"

"You want a promise? Okay, I promise." It was half-hearted at best.

"Yeah, we both know there's nothing keeping you to your word."

Bishop stood and turned to face me. "For what Beasley wants, this is how it works."

His patience was wearing, which was not ideal. And it was clear I had no power in the situation and no resources to play hardball.

Fine. Whatever. It was Donovan who'd be out cash if I returned empty-handed, something he surely knew when he made the deal. Goal was just to make sure *I* returned.

Whoa. That was new. Since when did I care about a potential risk to my life? My flippancy about death had been one of the reasons I'd been suited to this kind of job in the past.

I refused to let myself acknowledge when and why that had changed.

Keeping my senses on alert, I crossed to the desk, set the case down, and took a step back. Bishop bent to enter the combination. The lid flipped open, and he nodded to the guy who wasn't the bigwig saying, "Be sure it's all there."

I hadn't counted it in Donovan's office. It had been a lot, and I probably could have done some fast math if I'd wanted to, but I hadn't. Now that not-bigwig was thumbing through it, it was obvious just how much my friend was willing to hand over.

And it was a lot.

The minutes passed like hours as all the cash was counted and inspected with a digital light to be sure they were real and hadn't been marked. Finally, the goon announced it was all there and accounted for. "Plus $10K," he added.

I'd forgotten I was supposed to mention that. "That's a tip for the rush."

Bishop studied my face, as though he thought the extra

money might have been a trick. "No tip necessary. But we'll keep it for a down payment for future interactions." He nodded to his guy to take the cash to a large safe on the floor behind him.

I fidgeted as I watched the money get packed inside, then breathed a sigh of relief when the guy returned to Bishop with a hard drive. "Real sensitive info on here," he said, holding it up. "Hope Beasley knows what he's getting into."

Jesus, so did I.

"It's password protected." Bishop dropped the drive in the case. "He knows what it is. Any problems getting into it, he knows how to reach me."

The hard drive could be blank. It could all be a scam. But thirty more seconds, and I'd have what I came for. I'd be back on the street within two minutes.

Except, just as Bishop started to close the lid, a noise came from the hallway behind me. Footsteps and a shuffling sound like one of the people walking wasn't coming willingly.

I wasn't facing the door and didn't turn because it was never wise to take eyes off the man in charge. But I knew.

Maybe it was the scent of cherry blossoms.

Or the muffled high-pitched scream.

Or maybe just that I fucking knew Jolie, knew that she never took kindly to a no, knew that she was stubborn as the day was long.

Whatever it was that made me certain, I didn't have to look to know that when all the men in the room pulled their guns out in alarm, they were aiming them at her.

TWENTY-FOUR

"Found her sniffing around the back door," Burly Man from downstairs said.

"I was looking for my cat?"

I cringed at the sound of her voice—confirmation that it was her and the ridiculous lie, one she couldn't even make convincing with the question at the end.

I turned just enough so that I could see her without putting my back to Bishop, slowly so as not to arouse a reaction from any of the gun-wielding men. Seeing her was both a relief and an ache. She was in one piece, didn't seem scuffed up in any way.

But she had a gun to her head, and it took everything in me not to rip Burly Man's arms off his body for being the one to hold it there.

I focused on her face, trying to blot out the Glock pointed at her temple. She looked scared, which did something to my insides, but not scared enough, which did something to my brain. *Fuck, Jolie. Why didn't you just do what I asked, for your own damn good?*

As if she could hear my thoughts, she mouthed a *sorry*.

"She's with me," I said, knowing I'd probably just screwed Donovan's deal out of existence.

"With you?" Bishop had already removed the hard drive from the case. Now it sat open and empty, the object of our pursuit in the hands of the man who'd counted the money. "There were strict instructions that you come alone."

Jolie opened her mouth to say something, but I shot her a silencing look. "You know women. They never listen."

I addressed her now with false admonition that would be very real later, when we got out of this. If we got out of this. "You were supposed to wait at the hotel, baby. I told you I'd be back later." I added the endearment for the men—an indication that she wasn't a threat to whatever business these guys were doing—but also it was for her. To give her some reassurance in whatever way I knew how.

"I got impatient." Her voice was tinier now, her eyes wider as she scanned the room and really took in the situation. She practically shrank in front of me. "I think I probably made a mistake."

You think?

Bishop narrowed his eyes. "She's...what? Your wife?"

I knew this kind of questioning technique. I'd used it many times in the past. He'd already checked out our bare left hands. He was trying to catch us in a lie.

"Girlfriend," I said.

At the same time Jolie said, "Fiancée."

She wasn't helping. I was going to kill her later for trying.

"Girlfriend," I corrected. "Stop getting ahead of yourself,

baby. These men don't want to hear us get into another argument about it."

Except for the guy holding her, the others relaxed a bit, identifying with the nagging-lover trope, either for real or for show, as happens with men around their peers.

"If she's a problem, we could take her off your hands." It was the first time Bishop had smiled since I'd walked in the room, and now that he did, I saw I'd been mistaken in thinking he wasn't carrying. That smile was his own weapon, as threatening as any hardware.

Whatever he intended by the offer, it was clear that death would be the nicest of options.

I could hear my blood rushing in my ears. "I'll pass. I hate to say it in front of her, but I'm kind of attached."

He swept his eyes down her body, pausing too long at her curves. "Understandable." He stuck one hand into the pockets of his crisp suit pants and scratched at his bare chin with the other. "But you see, now we got a problem. You know what we do when someone doesn't follow the rules?"

He was going to tell me anyway, so I didn't answer. Thankfully, Jolie kept her mouth shut as well.

Again that evil smile. "Why don't you tell him, Ross?"

I looked to the goon who'd counted the money, thinking he must be who Bishop was addressing, but it turned out Ross was the burly man holding Jolie captive. "Sure, Bish. We shoot them."

Jolie let out an involuntary squeak. I saw the quiver in her lip just before she covered her mouth with her hand.

Finally, she was as scared as she ought to be.

It had been a long time, but now I was too. "All right, hold on. Let's not overreact here. She did something dumb. Real dumb. It wasn't intentional. Just let us go. You got our money. Let us walk out the door, empty-handed if you prefer. No harm, no foul, and you're up a lot of cash."

"I'm up the cash anyway." He was fully aware he held every card. But he did seem intrigued by something. "You're willing to walk out of here without Beasley's drive? That much money sent out with no prize in return, seems you'd be dead anyway."

Of course Bishop assumed that Donovan was my boss. He definitely didn't realize that I had twice the amount we'd handed over in my personal checking account.

All of which made me more of a threat than if I were simply an errand boy. In my eagerness to talk him down, I'd drawn suspicion. If we weren't worried about our lives, then who were we?

"No, no, no." Jolie's panic erupted before I'd thought through my next move. "We can't leave without the information, Cade. We have to—"

I winced as she used my real name. "Shut up, baby. I've got this handled." I didn't have this handled at all. I addressed Bishop. "Obviously, I'd rather we left with the drive. But if that's off the table, I'll take my chances with Beasley. At least that's not a sure step in the grave. But, really, do we need to be talking graves at all? For such a minor infraction, it doesn't seem like a reason to get blood on your hands."

On the outside, I was cool. As cool as I'd been the times I'd been the one throwing the threats. Nine times out of ten, that's exactly what they were—threats. Nothing more. Except for the extreme psychopaths and sadists—and there were far less in the underground than people imagined—no one actually wanted to exert force, no matter the form.

But I was the furthest thing from cool. Because that one time out of ten was enough to cry bad odds when Jolie was involved. Even as a kid shaking under the hand of Headmaster Stark, I'd never been this scared. Never felt this helpless. Never felt this on the verge of unleashing whatever beast lived locked up inside me.

They could do whatever they wanted to me. They could break me into a million impossible-to-identify pieces. But if they hurt one hair on Jolie's head...

I wasn't sure there was a word for the kind of fear-rage that inspired.

"He makes a point." The weaponized grin had been put away, but Bishop was still terrifying knowing it was in his pocket. "Lot of hassle, and probably not necessary. Especially since we've already been paid."

He considered a minute, then nodded to the money counter. "Put the drive back in the case." The goon did as he was told, then Bishop once again shut the lid. This time he entered the code locking the contents in place.

"You're letting us take it?" Rule number one in negotiating was not to sound unsure, and I'd fucking failed big time. It seemed too unlikely that we'd leave with the case. It still seemed unlikely that we'd leave at all.

"I am." Bishop took the case by the handle and stretched his arm forth, inviting me to take it.

I stretched my hand out, carefully, sure it was a trick.

It was.

As soon as my fingers were close to touching it, he pulled it back, out of reach. "But first, if we're going to let you two go, we have to be sure you aren't cops. I'm sure you understand. Ross, strip the lady. Check for a wire."

Without being told, like well-rehearsed choreography, one of the other men stepped in, pointing his gun so that Ross could pocket his and pull at Jolie's coat.

Renewed rage mingled with adrenaline-fueled panic surged through my veins. "Don't you fucking dare touch her!"

I rushed forward, only to be seized by two men, one at each arm.

And since Ross didn't take orders from me, he threw her removed coat to the floor and reached for the hem of her sweater.

"Please, don't." Jolie trembled, her arms folded across her chest as though that could ward him off. "Please. At least let me do it myself. I can show you I'm not wearing a wire."

That wasn't much better, but at least she wouldn't have their wretched hands on her.

"No can do," Ross said, immediately squashing that idea. "Who knows? You might have something hiding beneath all your clothes."

The way he said it made it very clear that Ross knew exactly what was under her clothes, and that was exactly what he planned to get his hands on.

"Don't fucking touch her!" I fought against the men holding me, almost breaking free before my arm was wrenched painfully behind my back.

Bishop chuckled, clearly amused. "You really are attached to her, aren't you? Maybe you should give her that ring she's after."

I flailed again, already planning Bishop's death. I'd slit his throat as soon as I finished ending Ross with a bullet between the eyes.

"You know what? I get it. I got a lady I like too. Cut it, Ross.

Entertaining as this is, we should probably be respectful to Beasley's man if we want to do business with him again."

Ross hadn't gotten far with the sweater, thank God, and he stepped away immediately without arguing.

I didn't have time to examine whether or not I could trust this change of heart before he showed me that I couldn't.

"We do need to be sure she's not wearing a wire, though." Bishop almost sounded apologetic about it. "So I'm willing to let you conduct the search yourself."

"She's not wearing a goddamned wire," I said.

He ignored me. "Ross, bring the lady here so *Cade* can show us his woman's clean."

I didn't even blanch at the acknowledgment that he'd caught my name. I was too concerned with her, with what I was being asked to do to her.

Not asked. Told. There was no option for me to say no.

It was a game. That much was obvious. If it had been unacceptable for Jolie to undress herself, it should have been unacceptable for me to do it in her place. The whole thing was just some asshole power trip.

And it didn't matter. In this scenario, she and I held none of the power.

It was almost like being back in high school.

"I'm sorry," I said quietly, when Ross brought Jolie in front of me. "I'm going to have to."

"I know." Her throat sounded clogged with tears. "It's okay. It's my fault."

It *was* her fault, but I felt responsible too. For no good reason, except that I would have to do this to her. My insides were an aluminum can under the stamp of a foot. I was sure I looked misshapen on the outside, like everyone in the room could tell that I'd been sufficiently crushed. It was impossible that it wasn't obvious. I was pretty sure that was the entire point.

After a series of warnings, my arms were released. I cupped her cheek with my hand, a comforting gesture that likely held little weight considering our predicament.

"Nothing funny," Ross warned, pulling his gun back out. Now there were two pointed at us, and the men who'd held me only feet away, ready to grab me again if necessary.

Taking a deep breath, I took the edge of her sweater in my hands and gently pulled it over her head. She reached her arms out to help me, and I wanted to kiss her for that—for being cooperative. For trusting me. For realizing there was no other choice.

Those weren't the only reasons I wanted to kiss her.

I could admit that here, under these circumstances, when that desire that had seemed so overwhelmingly frightening hours before suddenly felt like the least terrifying emotion I'd had all day. I threw her sweater to the floor and moved to the button on her jeans, promising myself that, if we made it through this, I would deal with this feeling head-on. I would even look forward to it.

I had the denim pushed down her thighs before I remembered her boots. I knelt down on the ground before her, wondering if later, when I could laugh about this, I'd find the humor in the fact that I'd been right when I'd worried she'd have me on my knees soon enough.

This hadn't been quite what I'd envisioned when the thought had crossed my mind, and then again, wasn't it exactly what I should have expected? Because this was where I'd always been drawn to. Because she'd always been my master and I a groveling servant at her feet who would lay down my life for hers if required.

I prayed it was only her clothes that would be asked for. I knew I'd give everything I owned if it wasn't.

After her boots, I removed her socks. Then her jeans came off, and she was standing in the chilly room wearing nothing but her bra and the damn cotton panties that had teased me all week.

I stood up, rubbing my hands along her goosebump-riddled arms.

"See. No wire." I didn't take my gaze off hers, conscious that she was half naked and that I was the only one still looking at her eyes.

"Need to see inside her bra," Bishop insisted. I knew he would, but I had to try.

"Need to see that pussy too," Ross said, his pants already tenting.

I bit the insides of my cheeks until I tasted blood.

"It's okay," she said again, trying to comfort me. But her eyes were spilling, and I knew that as strong as she was trying to be, she was the one who needed the comfort.

"Pretend it's just you and me." I spoke softly, but not too quietly, knowing it wasn't wise to appear like we were plotting something. I reached behind her and undid the clasp of her bra. "Just you and me, back at the hotel."

She nodded, her focus pinned right on me so I could count each and every tear that trickled down her cheek.

"We're alone," I continued as I pulled the straps down her arms, "and this moment is ours. We've waited so long for this. *I've* waited so long. And now we've reached the place where it's impossible to wait any longer."

Her bra was off, her breasts fully exposed to a room full of leering men.

They were there, but they weren't. We were in our own bubble, she and I, and as naked as she was, I was on the verge of baring more.

That seemed about right. That seemed exactly right.

"It feels like I'm underwater with you," I said as I tugged her panties past her hips, my fingers trembling as they brushed against her skin. "And there's a very good chance that I'm gonna drown. But sink or swim, baby. I'm holding on to you this time for dear life."

And now she was completely stripped.

And the way her face crumpled, the way her eyes remained only on mine—I was pretty sure she knew I was stripped too.

"Look at that. No wire," Ross said, amusement in his tone, a blunt reminder that her vulnerability was much more real than mine.

Instinctively, I moved to cover her as well as I could.

"Maybe we need to examine her a little more closely," someone else said.

Fortunately for him, before I could knock the man's eyes out, consequences be damned, Bishop had tired of the game. He went back to the desk, his back turned to me as he perched again on the edge. "Let her get dressed. Take your case, Cade, and get the fuck out of here. You've already wasted more of my night than I'd planned."

He was done with me, done with us, demonstrating with his quick readiness to move on that this whole charade had been nothing but a show of power. He hadn't even bothered to check me.

But I wasn't going to challenge him.

While Jolie pulled on her underwear, I retrieved her coat. She put her jeans on, then let me put her boots on her feet, not bothering with socks, while she pulled the sweater over her head. When she just had her coat to deal with, I crossed to grab the case.

"Beasley knows where to find me if he needs anything else." Bishop didn't look up as he delivered his parting words. "But also make sure he knows that any trouble that comes down from poking into this is his and his alone."

I didn't bother with a response. Grabbing the briefcase, I took Jolie's hand in the other and pulled her with me out of the room, down the stairs, and into the night, racing as though we could outrun any trouble that followed.

Wondering if she was as aware as I was that everything had changed.

TWENTY-FIVE

We didn't stop moving until we were getting into a cab. I'd been shaken, and even now, sure that we'd left with our lives, I felt precariously held together. As much as I wanted to discover what was on the hard drive—if there was anything at all—I couldn't deal with Donovan until I'd had some time to unwind.

Knowing he'd be anxious, I sent him a quick text.

Got the case. I'll meet up with you in the morning.

His reply came instantly. **I can meet you at the hotel in thirty.**

Not tonight, D.

He'd know better not to push me, but I turned off my phone all the same.

"I didn't think it through," Jolie said when I'd pocketed my cell. "The taxi stopped at a light, and I saw you on the sidewalk, and I just...I just got out and followed you."

"We don't need to do this right now."

She went on as if I hadn't said anything. "I knew you didn't need my help. But I couldn't stand the thought of leaving you alone. Not again."

I closed my eyes, a blanket of exhaustion covering me. I didn't have strength in me to deal with these words. I didn't feel equipped to keep the flicker of hope from turning into a full-fledged flame. "I don't want to talk about it."

She didn't say anything after that, simply stared out the window, her expression unreadable, and it wasn't until we were halfway to our destination that it occurred to me that I'd been an asshole. *Too much* of an asshole. And if I'd learned anything from today, it was that I didn't actually want to be that with her.

"Hey, Jol? Are you okay?" My fingers were still threaded in hers, which I only just noticed, and now that I had, it was impossible not to be completely aware of it.

She turned her face from the window and blinked a few times, as though she were struggling to put me in focus. "Yeah. I think I am." She glanced down at our clasped hands, and when her eyes returned to the glass, I almost thought I caught a smile on her lips.

We stayed silent for the rest of the ride, our hands linked, until we got to the hotel, and I had to free myself to manage my wallet. Outside of the cab, I reached for her again, automatically. Like I'd done it a hundred times before.

She gave me her hand, but while I continued walking toward the hotel doors, she stopped, pulling me back toward her.

"Cade." Her expression was earnest, and I sensed an urgency in her, as though she feared that whatever she had to say couldn't be said once we passed from the cold night to the warmth of the lobby.

Or maybe she feared this truce we'd come to wouldn't last past the threshold of the doors.

To be honest, I feared that too.

But not as much as I feared what she was about to say. "Don't," I warned.

She held me tighter, grabbing my wrist with her other hand, and though I could easily pull free, I felt caught. Like a water pipe tangled in tree roots. A hard thing, hollow on the inside, unable to escape from this living intrusion.

Stay hard, I willed myself. *Stay hollow.*

"I didn't want—"

"Don't!" It was harsher this time. A threat.

"I didn't want you to leave me," she said, bulldozing through the words before I could cut her off again.

I stared at her, trying very hard to be that hard, hollow thing, knowing that she wasn't talking about tonight. Knowing these words could change everything if I let them. *Everything.*

And fuck if that didn't make me want to hit something.

Because no. She couldn't do this. It wasn't fair. She couldn't disappear for seventeen years and then show up all vulnerable and soft and unchanged and then try to change the narrative that she herself had written. A narrative that had made me what I was now. Cold and rigid and empty.

She had no right.

I yanked my hand away from her, knowing a physical escape wouldn't do any good. It didn't even matter that she followed as I stormed through the hotel doors, or that she would be in the suite with me upstairs. I could put a thousand miles between us, and I still wouldn't have outrun this.

Didn't mean I wasn't going to try.

I walked through the lobby with long strides that her shorter legs couldn't match. When she caught up with me waiting for the elevator, I ignored her, as though she were some random woman with no ties to me other than the fact that she was in my vicinity.

She gave me my space, quietly occupying the opposite side of the car, allowing me to ignore her existence, though it was possible she was reciprocating. And if she was, fine. I didn't care. I watched the numbers for each floor light as we went up, up, up, and focused on forcing every bit of consciousness into that one action so that there weren't any brain cells left for caring. Or analyzing or recalibrating. Or wondering what would happen if I stopped running. Stopped trying to escape. Stopped searching for closure.

I didn't wait for her to exit first when we reached our floor, ignoring the male rules of etiquette and stomping to our suite so far ahead of her that the door had almost closed behind me when she caught it and pushed in.

And when she did, as soon as I heard the movement of air as the door swept open, I dropped the case and turned, crossing toward her, so that by the time it did click closed, I had already taken her in my arms.

"You're going to wreck me all over again," I said before crashing my lips against hers, which wasn't really true because she'd already wrecked me all over again, and now I was pretty sure she was doing the opposite—putting me together. Finding jagged pieces of me that had seemed to have no place for so long, and matching them with uneven pieces of her. Fitting us perfectly together with her presence. And her patience. And her lips.

God, her lips.

Kissing her was both familiar and new. A dance I'd forgotten. I anticipated the tilt of her head, the flick of her tongue. The soft sigh in the back of her throat as I became more aggressive.

If she'd been surprised by my attack, she only showed eagerness and urgency that matched my own. She tasted like want and mint. Like that candy that I loved years ago that they didn't make anymore. She tasted like refuge and peace, and kissing her was like going home.

Which was surreal considering that I'd never thought I'd go home again.

I wasn't sure who started pushing at clothing first, but both our coats fell to the floor quickly. Her hands slipped under my sweater, her palms hot against my bare chest as she kissed along my neck.

I returned the favor, savoring the salty taste of her skin and marveling at her rapid pulse underneath my tongue. It beat in tandem with the bass drum at the center of my torso, and part of me wanted to bite into her flesh and rip at her artery as if that would end this connection that existed between us. That twisted, perverted bond that should never have been born.

But that was only a very small part of me. The bigger part wanted to endure the fate of our bond, would enjoy it even if it destroyed me.

With one arm wrapped tightly around her waist, I slid the other down over her ass and squeezed the plump curve. She was rounder here than she'd been when we were young, and I loved it. I wanted to learn this change. Wanted to memorize the new landscape of her body. I squeezed again, harder. Then, angry at the barrier of her jeans, I swatted her with my palm.

Impatiently, I undid her pants, only bothering to push them down to her knees. I needed her ass, needed her flesh in my hands, needed it so urgently that I didn't even try to take off her panties. I just pushed through the leg holes until I had a cheek in each hand and gripped tightly, peering over her shoulder at the erotic sight.

Damn, she felt good. Supple and pliable and, Jesus, I could become obsessed with this ass. I could make a full-time job of fondling and massaging and licking and fucking this gorgeous round ass.

This time when I spanked her, I was angry at myself. For wanting her so much. For letting her exceed my expectations. For being so goddamned fascinated with my reddened palm print on her ass. I slapped her again, sharply. And again.

She squealed at each strike, a sound that called directly to my already stiff cock, making him stand up as though Jolie was his drill sergeant, calling him to attention. He was ready to take her. He wanted nothing more than to bury into her pussy, reclaim her. Get lost there. Lose control.

But there was a risk to feeling so wild. Especially with her.

In an attempt to find my balance, I pushed her against the wall, startling her lips from my skin. I placed my hands at either side of her neck, fingers spread, and lifted her chin with my thumbs, then looked directly into her hooded eyes.

The thing was, me and Jolie—we were more complicated than a quick fuck or even a long fuck. I'd been a hypocrite calling her out for being someone who turned sex into something more. Anything that happened between us *had* to be more than just physical, not only because that was what I wanted, but because there wasn't any other way with her. With us. We'd always been more than what we should have been. It had been our curse.

It had been our fortune too.

I needed to know if she understood what this would be before it got too far to redefine. My mouth hovered inches above hers, our lips parted, and tried to stare into her. Was there any of what we used to be still inside her? Or was all of this one-sided? Was I carrying this fucked up torch on my own?

I wanted answers to questions I couldn't bring myself to ask, hoping I wouldn't have to. Hoping she'd just know, and I'd know in return.

But while I was searching her eyes, she brought her hand to the steel pole in my jeans and rubbed up and down the length with a pressure that made me insane, and after that, I couldn't concentrate on worrying about what this was or what this wasn't. My thoughts descended into a primal state, and all hopes of staying tame disappeared.

In a flash, her sweater was gone. Unlike when I'd removed it earlier, this time I gave all my focus to what was underneath, desperately kissing along the skin above her bra while my hands reached behind to undo the clasp. When the garment fell off her shoulders, I caught her breasts with my palms and plumped them a little harder than I should, unable to restrain myself.

She leaned into my touch and moaned, her fingers wrapping into my sweater and clinging for stability, and all I could think was *it's about fucking time*. It was her turn to be off-balance. Her turn to be reeling.

And bonus that she seemed to like the rough because I didn't think there was much chance I could be any other way. There was too much pent up inside of me. Too many years of longing. Too much resentment. Too much hate that might have been love or love that might have been hate, and I needed her to feel all of it, whether she understood it or not.

I pinched at a nipple, twisting it until she gasped, then tortured it with soft strokes of my tongue, then moved to her other breast and took that peak by my teeth, clamping down until she jerked back with a cry.

Even as she pulled away, she begged for more.

I'd imagined her pleading a million times, usually with my cock in my fist and my eyes shut tight. I hadn't been able to rely on memory for this. We'd been inexperienced lovers when we'd first been together, our sex talk sweet and awkward, matching the actual sex. I'd been long gone by the time my desires had turned dirtier, and when I'd placed her in my fantasies, she'd adjusted to fit my wants.

But my imaginings had never been half as tantalizing as the real thing—her eyes tearing, her lips swollen and quivering, her cheeks flushed as she cried, "Please, Cade. Please. Please, fuck me. Please, please, please."

As though we'd orchestrated it, while she pulled down her panties to join her jeans at her knees, I took the three steps to the minibar and grabbed what we needed, grateful for the modern-day hotel custom of stocking condoms.

Back in front of her, I ripped open the foil square while she unfastened my pants. She brought out my cock, her hands small and dainty compared to the red, veined stick she held. I handed her the condom and half watched her roll it on, half took in her half-naked state.

Earlier, in a room full of men who only wanted to objectify her, I'd wanted to be the one man to respect her. I'd been careful to only look at her eyes. Now I soaked up every inch of her like she was a Playboy centerfold, letting every lewd impulse have free rein of my mind. Her full, fuckable tits would feel spectacular in my hands. I could feast on her trim pussy. I could lick up the moisture glistening on her lips or gather it on my fingers to lube up her ass. I could use her and fuck her and destroy her in so many ways that she deserved. In so many ways that she didn't.

But then my gaze returned to her face, to the eyes that windowed into the soul of a woman that I would never stop crawling toward. She had a noose around my neck, leading me like a dog, and faithful pet that I was, I would always come back seeking her love, whether she was done with me or not.

Did she know? Did she have any idea at all?

She rose up on her tiptoes to brush her lips to mine. If she kissed me now, there would be no hiding. No more pretense. No way to hold back.

Not ready for that level of vulnerability, I refused her kiss and spun her around so she faced the wall. So she didn't face me. Reaching between her legs, I made sure she was as wet and ready as she'd looked, then when she pushed her ass back and begged again, this time for my cock, I notched my crown at the mouth of her pussy and drove in.

Being inside her, after all this time, was indescribable. Neither of us were the same. Our bodies had changed. Our behavior had changed.

And still there was an easiness to our fit. A rhythm that didn't have to be learned. Filthy as it was—her cheek pressed against the wall as I pounded into her, the slapping of our thighs, the gasping cries tumbling from her lips, the butterfly pulses of her pussy around my cock—it was far from the innocent lovemaking of our youth. I'd never fucked her like this. We'd never *fucked* at all.

And still, she was Jolie. She was *my* Jolie, and every part of my body acknowledged the difference between her and every other woman I'd been with. None compared to her. None were anything like this.

I tried to forget that and lose myself in *just another pussy*, an impossible task when she craned her head around in an attempt to recapture my lips. She managed a brief kiss that had my legs feeling like they might give out. That had my chest feeling like it might explode.

Capturing her hands, I turned her again to face the wall. I kept her like that, my fingers threaded through hers, holding her in place so I could fuck her with abandon while she alternated between pleading not to stop and begging for more.

Then her litany changed. "Touch me, Cade. Please, I need you to touch me." It wasn't only the words that were different in these pleas, but the texture of their sound. They were thin and stretched, like it had taken a lot to ask. Like she'd wanted to be selfless. Like she'd thought there was a reward in keeping her needs to herself, but finally, she couldn't stand it anymore and gave in to her craving.

There was a version of me that wanted to deny her pleasure. Not in a kinky, fun way, but in a way that made her feel insignificant and used.

But I was as selfish as she was, and I wanted to hear her come, wanted to feel her pussy squeeze me tight, wanted to make sure she remembered this fuck and that she got wet whenever she did.

So I moved one hand to pinch her tit and the other to rub between her legs.

It didn't take much after that. A minute or two of watching her cues, learning what got her going, then teasing her with that pressure while I drove into her over and over and over, until the painting began to thump against the wall, until I was sure the neighboring suite would call management to complain. Then, on a "Yes, Cade, fuck yes," her entire body stuttered, and her pussy clamped down on my cock.

The pressure and the flood of wet heat sent me tumbling after her, surprising me with the sudden intensity. I came long and hard, as though I'd stored it up for her. As though it had been years instead of days since I'd last released. As though there was no part of me that I wouldn't give my all of, and my cock knew that score, even if my head didn't.

Seemed about right.

Breathless, I pulled out of her. Stepped back until I was leaning against the counter by the bar. My pants hung at my hips, my cock sticking out, as hard and thick as before I'd entered her. I removed the condom, tying it off and throwing it in the trash nearby, and then I dared to look at Jolie.

She'd turned around, but her pants were still around her knees, her breasts still exposed, her face and chest flushed. Her face glistening with sweat.

She was fucking beautiful.

I wanted her all over again.

"Should we talk about this?" she asked, and I could tell from her inflection that she was leaving it up to me—what came next, what was said, what wasn't.

And I thought of all the things I'd wanted to tell her over the years, the things I needed her to know. The feelings that I was sure could only be sorted with her help.

And I thought about the way I hadn't been able to breathe

when she'd shown up at that meeting, how it physically hurt to think what might happen to her. And I thought about the case. The secrets it held inside. The task I'd promised to help her do.

I thought about what day it was. Thought about the flight she'd board tomorrow, how she'd get on a plane. How soon I would be getting on a plane too, but my flight path would take me to the other side of the world.

I glanced at the bar next to me, saw there were three more condoms in the pack. "I'd rather do that again." I nodded toward her, so she'd have no doubt what "that" meant.

"Just once?"

I held up the condoms. "Or more."

"This time in a bed?"

I nodded. "This time without any clothes."

"Yeah, I can get behind that."

So I took her hand, led her to my bed, and pretended that the memories from a night of fucking could possibly fill the cavity she'd leave tomorrow when she flew away.

TWENTY-SIX

I squatted next to the bed and studied her sleeping features. Her face was soft, her lips curled into an almost smile. The small lines that indicated her age when she was awake were missing, and she looked more like the girl I'd fallen in love with than ever.

Spending an entire night with her in my bed had been surreal. I usually didn't let my conquests stay that long, and if they did, it was usually accidental—I'd been too drunk to push them out or the woman had already fallen asleep. I couldn't remember when I'd woken up to a woman that I'd invited to stay, if ever.

I hadn't just invited Jolie to stay—I hadn't let her out of my arms.

And there was the fact that she wasn't just any woman. She was *the* woman. Even with the proof of her in front of me, her naked chest rising and falling with the rhythmic breaths of sleep, it felt very much like a dream. The best dream.

I didn't want to wake up.

She stirred, a sigh passed her lips, and while I very much wanted to leave her to whatever was happening in her head, there was a clock ticking.

I swept a strand of her blonde hair off her face, noting her natural light brown coming in at the roots. "Hey, Jol."

Her eyelids fluttered, but she didn't open them.

I brushed my knuckles across her cheek, using the excuse of waking her gently as a chance to touch her. This did the trick.

"Hi," she yawned. The room was mostly dark, a lone beam of sun streaming through a crack in the blackout curtains the only indication that morning had occurred. She frowned all the same when she realized I wasn't in the bed with her. "You're dressed."

"Early riser. Bad habit."

She chuckled, and my cock twitched.

I told him to calm the fuck down. He'd gotten to run the better part of the night. In the daylight, there were other priorities. Much as I'd rather ignore them, they didn't go away. "What time is your flight?"

Her frown returned, and she pulled the sheet up to cover her breasts, as though she just now realized that what we were to each other this morning was likely not what we were to each other last night.

"Um. Five fifteen." I hoped her sullen tone meant she was as unhappy about the countdown as I was.

But we had time. Not a lot, but some. "You should leave here no later than two. We need to get the case opened before that. Sooner the better." Whatever the contents showed, we'd have to make a plan of where we went from here.

Where we went regarding her father, anyway.

I wasn't holding any hopes that there would be a conversation about the future of anything else. "Donovan should be in the office in half an hour. Do you want to go with me, or do you want to keep sleeping?"

"I want to come."

I stayed crouched at her side. Glad as I was that she'd be with me, I felt guilty for the faint circles under her eyes. "You didn't get much sleep. I'm sorry I kept you up."

"I'm not." Her cheeks pinkened, bold as she was.

I figured I'd only gotten about three hours of sleep myself, and I wasn't sorry either. Not one bit. If she hadn't looked so thoroughly exhausted the last time I'd made her come, I would have kept her up longer.

"You're not sorry either, are you?" It was more of a statement than a question, but I sensed her need to be sure.

I answered by leaning forward and pressing my mouth to hers.

What was meant to be a light, affirming kiss quickly turned into my hand sliding under the sheet in search of the warmth between her legs, and it was only the moan that escaped against my lips that brought me to my senses.

I pulled my hand away and broke off abruptly. "We'll lose the whole day if we get started."

Her mischievous smile said that wouldn't be the worst thing in the world.

"Uh-uh." I pushed up to my feet, hoping to eliminate temptation with distance. Also, to give my cock a little breathing room.

She widened her grin, her gaze planted squarely on the evidence of my arousal. "Not that I'm complaining, but I'd say you've got the stamina of a teenager if I knew for a fact that you weren't like this as a teen."

I tensed automatically, the way I always seemed to when we started talking about before. Despite what had happened between us last night, our past was still a minefield that had to be navigated carefully. It was easier to leave it alone altogether.

But something had changed between us. Because this time I didn't back away. "Given the chance back then, I would have fucked us both raw. I didn't have the opportunity."

"No, we didn't." Her blush was back, which didn't help the state of my cock. "I need a shower. Want to join me?"

We probably had time for whatever her offer would likely turn into. Considering we were out of condoms, a shower made sense. Pulling out would be easy cleanup.

God, I was tempted.

But losing time wasn't the only thing at risk. The transition to today's relationship status would only be harder if we tried to prolong last night's status. And I was already struggling with trying to figure out what was between us—what was new, what was old, what didn't matter, what did. I still carried very real wounds where she was concerned, and while the sex had been an incredible and much-needed distraction from the pain, it didn't mean those injuries were healed.

Maybe some of them were.

Maybe most of them were.

They certainly didn't feel as present today. Figured, didn't it? That just as I'd abandoned my need for closure, my wounds might finally be closed. Maybe that was exactly how closure worked.

I needed to work that out, and getting filthy in the shower was only going to cloud that analysis.

"You're thinking about it too hard," she said, climbing out of the bed with no concern for her nudity. "I'm going to jump in, and if you join me, you join me. If not, I'm not going to take it personally."

As always, she was less fucked up about us than I was. For once, I didn't resent her for it.

Progress.

But I forced myself to let her shower alone all the same.

BY THE TIME we arrived at Reach an hour later, we'd fully transitioned to our new status, whatever that was. I was able to look at her without wanting to bend her over every available piece of furniture, though maybe that was because I really wasn't looking at her very much. It was easier this way, with distance between us.

The hard part was not being bitter about it, but I was trying my best not to be an asshole.

Jolie, as always, seemed to be letting me have my space, which I appreciated. Though I wouldn't have minded if she'd stood a little closer in the elevator or reached for my hand when we walked down the hall to Donovan's office, especially when we got to Simone's desk. Stupid as it was, I would have preferred to face her under the guise of being off-limits, for no other reason than that I liked the idea of being off-limits because I belonged to Jolie.

I obviously still had work to do on the whole letting go thing.

"He hasn't arrived yet, but he'll be in shortly," Simone said, completely professional. As though she hadn't had her hands down my pants days before.

That was odd since it was a quarter to nine. Donovan was generally in before eight, and I'd messaged him that we'd be here.

Simone came around her desk and headed to his office, a key in hand. "He said you could wait in here. Can I get you anything? Coffee? Latte? Muffins?"

"We're good." I shooed her off as soon as she had the door unlocked. When it was closed behind us, I set the briefcase on Donovan's desk and apologized to Jolie. "I suppose I should have let you answer before sending Simone away."

"I'm happier with her gone. Thanks."

I'd seen her jealous before, years ago. When I'd made a spectacle of myself with another girl in an attempt to try to distract myself from the very forbidden Julianna Stark. She'd had the same upward tilt of her chin, the same triumphant gleam in her eye when I'd ended that mockery of a relationship as she did now.

Fuck if it didn't make me want to kiss the hell out of her.

I settled for taking her coat and then getting her a bottle of sparkling water from the mini fridge. Only when I sat down in the chair next to her and a few silent minutes had passed did I notice the cloud of things we needed to say hanging in the air between us.

Coward that I was, I ignored it.

But Jolie had always been braver. "Since we might not get the chance later...something should probably be said."

Her awkward approach encouraged me to grow some balls. If she could be hesitant and still take on the minefield, then so could I.

"Look, um." I leaned forward, bracing my elbows on my thighs, steepling my tattooed hands together. "I've been unreasonable. Holding you responsible for the past. We were kids. Holding a grudge for something that occurred when we were teens..." I cleared my throat. "I apologize for being immature."

I hadn't been facing her while I talked—because, chickenshit—but now I turned my head to her. The corners of her mouth weren't exactly turned down, but her forehead was wrinkled, as though she found what I'd said troubling, or at the very least, puzzling. "Is that what that was? Immaturity?"

"On my part, yes. What else would it be?"

"I was hoping it was..." With a shake of her head, she let out an embarrassed sort of laugh. "I guess I was hoping it meant you still had some sort of feelings for me. Ridiculous after all these years. After what I did. I'm the immature one it seems."

Just like that, everything stopped. My heart. The clock. The air in my lungs.

If she'd been hoping I had some sort of feelings for her, did that mean that she had some sort of feelings for me?

I was half a second away from pouring out every emotion I still very much felt for her when Donovan rushed through the door.

"You have the case?" He saw it on his desk before I had a chance to answer. "I'm a bit late coming in. Sabrina and I are leaving early today for Washington, and I needed to get some things taken care of on the way in so that our weekend would be possible."

"Going home?" I asked, knowing that Washington, Connecticut was where he grew up and seemed the more likely location for a getaway than Washington state, especially in the middle of December.

Though taking the girlfriend to meet the parents meant the guy was in deeper than I'd realized.

"Don't say it," he said, correctly guessing that I'd been about to mock him. He threw his coat on the back of his chair and reached for the case, but before he opened it he studied us, his eyes darting from me to Jolie to me again. "You're in no position to talk."

I felt my face heating although, seriously, there was no way he could know shit. Not just from glancing at us.

Moving on, he opened the briefcase and retrieved the hard drive. After a quick inspection—which, what? Did he think it might be a bomb?—he plugged it into his computer and sat down at his desk.

"These guys you had me hook up with..." I said, remembering I hadn't talked to him at all about the insanity of the meeting. "Don't be surprised if that hard drive is blank."

"It's not going to be blank." He was more sure than he should be, in my opinion.

While he booted his computer, Jolie turned to me. "Did you tell him—?"

"That's a more in-depth conversation than I want to have at the moment." Mostly I was protecting her. I was sure he'd lay into Jolie if he knew she'd been there.

But later, I'd be sure to tell them these dudes were scary.

Of course Donovan missed nothing. He stopped typing. "What happened?"

I waved him off. "Not now. Let's just see if it was worth it."

He frowned, his expression skeptical. Then his curiosity about the contents of the drive seemed to overtake his curiosity about the meeting, and he turned his attention to the screen.

My own curiosity got me out of my chair and circling his

desk to peer behind him. He located the hard drive on the search panel, clicked it, then paused before entering the password. "Do you mind?"

I did mind. Very much. After what we'd been through to get the stupid thing.

But that was Donovan, with his secrets and his need for control. I wandered back to the other side of the desk where Jolie was now standing too.

"Maybe it's porn," she said, not bothering to lower her voice. "Kinky-ass porn."

"Like with horses, you think?"

"Furries. Guaranteed."

Donovan shot us a look, but I could tell he wasn't entirely unamused. "The drive's not empty," he said. "And the folder with the info I'd asked for is on it."

He clicked his mouse, and I came around again to look over his shoulder, propping my arm on the desk as I leaned in. A second later, I felt Jolie pressing against my back, and I lifted my arm so she could come in front of me. When I lowered my arm again, my hand landed on her back.

Purposely.

As always, touching her was distracting, but what was on the screen was compelling enough to grab my attention. A list of Word docs showed up in the directory, each with strange names.

F-17-V-09
F-17-V-11
M-16-U-11
F-15-V-07
F-16-U-04

· · ·

THE LIST WENT on and on. Twenty-five of them? Thirty, maybe.

The codes meant nothing to me, yet I had a bad feeling all the same.

"Click on one," Jolie said.

Instead, Donovan changed the view. A preview opened up, and now there was an image of a teenage girl I'd never seen and a bunch of stats—height, weight, hair color, birthdate, dollar amounts.

He scrolled down to the next doc which had similar info. And the next, this time a teenage boy.

"The M and F are their gender. And the first number is their age." Jolie was figuring out the code of the document titles.

Donovan scrolled down again.

"I recognize her." Her eyes scanned the info. "She disappeared soon after I graduated. That last number is the year she went missing."

Donovan scrolled to the next. And the next. And the next. All held similar images, similar stats, similar dollar amounts.

"There's Bernard Arnold," I said when we got to the boy who'd gone missing the year I'd been there. When Jolie identified more of the pictures as students that had disappeared from Stark Academy, it was clear. "These are missing person reports."

All that identifying info, the kind that had once been seen on the back of milk cartons, it couldn't be anything else. And the dollar amounts had to be rewards offered for the teens' return.

Very high dollar amounts. Impressively high.

"Didn't you already recognize the pattern of runaways

from researching public information? Why pay all that money for missing person reports?" Jolie's question was fair, though I suspected we weren't looking at just any reports. These were standardized. Organized. Like someone had broken into the FBI.

Donovan scrolled down again. "That's not what we're looking at."

Jolie looked back at me, her brow raised. I shrugged. When Donovan scrolled down again without saying more, I went ahead and asked. "Then what are we looking at?"

"Receipts."

The hair stood up on the back of my neck. "What do you mean receipts?"

"I mean exactly that," he said impatiently. "These are receipts. Bills of sale. Every one of them. These missing teens? They've been sold."

TWENTY-SEVEN

"Sold? Are you talking sex slavery?" Jolie sounded dubious, as though she thought Donovan was trying to sell us a conspiracy theory, and she was not buying.

If he was offended by being doubted, he didn't say. "Primarily, yes. Drug mules too. Whatever suits their owner's fancy."

She blinked. "You can't *own* a person."

"Unfortunately, some people believe you can," Donovan said.

"And you think my father is one of those people?"

Donovan and I exchanged a glance. Stark certainly had the opportunity. Even if he wasn't already my enemy number one, he would be the first person I'd look at given the evidence.

Our lack of response said everything, and guessing from her reaction, it wasn't what Jolie wanted to hear. "How do you know that's what this is? Who told you that? This could be what Cade said it was. This could be someone making a scandal out of nothing."

The way we planned to make a scandal out of nothing?

I didn't say it, though, because Jolie was obviously having a hard time processing the depth of the crimes we were talking about.

Donovan excelled at remaining objective. "It's possible. I haven't worked with Bishop before, but I trust those who recommended him."

"Is this Bishop guy part of this?" I asked. "People don't have these records without being involved."

"He has a membership to a pleasure island in the Caribbean where these kinds of deals are done on the regular. My understanding is that Bishop made a deal of his own to get these records—apparently there is a member of the ring that he's been blackmailing with this."

It dawned on me that the scope of our plans had changed. "This doesn't just involve Stark anymore."

"No. It doesn't."

"You're serious about this." Jolie looked from me to Donovan, understanding sinking in. "You're really saying these teens didn't run away. That they were abducted. That they were sold."

Again, silence was as good of an answer as anything else.

She blinked a few more times, her eyes darting as she absorbed the situation. Then she sank down in a chair and brought her hand up to her mouth. "Oh my God. The V stands for virgin."

The tingly sensation at the top of my spine said she was right. "The U then?"

Donovan rubbed his chin. "Undetermined?"

Jolie's color had left her face. "I'm going to throw up."

In a flash, Donovan grabbed the trash can from under his desk and handed it to me. I started to pass it over, but she shook her head. "Not really. I don't think."

I moved behind her and rubbed my hand over the muscles at her neck.

She tilted her head toward me. "Do you really think he could do this?"

Did I think Headmaster Stark was so vile that he'd traffic teens out of his school? Given my feelings toward the man, it deserved a moment to consider. It would be easy to say yes because I hated him. Because I wanted to believe the worst of him. Because I wanted to bring him down.

But just because he beat kids on the regular didn't mean he'd try to sell them into slavery.

Then again, Stark's crimes against me had gone further than simply losing his temper. I had no doubt that his morals, if he had any at all, were flexible enough to lower himself to this level.

"You do, don't you?" she guessed when I hesitated.

I didn't want to bullshit her. But I cared about being sensitive. "I think someone did this. And if your father is in any way involved, he needs to be stopped. He needs to pay for it."

"And if you did want to destroy him, this stuff is pretty damning," Donovan piped in.

"If he's not responsible though..." I could sense she was working out her own morals as she spoke. "Can I really pin *this* on him? Of course, five days ago I was ready to kill him myself. Why does that seem easier to reconcile?"

"Because that was just between you and him. Now there

are other victims who can't fight him themselves. It's a lot of responsibility."

My hand dropped as she swiveled in her chair to face me. "Yes. That's exactly it."

Donovan let a beat pass, giving us time to absorb. "Obviously, this isn't information we can just ignore. Something has to be done with it. At this point, you're welcome to walk away. I can submit this to someone who will make sure a full investigation is opened up. We have to get someone rescuing these kids."

"They aren't kids anymore." My stomach churned thinking of how long these people had been missing. How many years of torture they'd endured. What that would do to a person. Were they even savable anymore?

"The point is that it needs to be stopped." I could tell from Donovan's tone that there was something he hadn't yet said. Something we hadn't yet thought of.

I tried to see what he was seeing. "So we can walk away, you take this to authorities, the whole ring comes down including Stark, and we don't have to have our hands in it at all?"

"Not exactly." He backpedaled. "I mean, I hope that's what happens. But this network has been running for a long time now. It's plainly very organized. Very well sheltered. It's possible authorities already know about it—I'd be more surprised if they didn't. Knowing about it doesn't mean it's easy to take down. These receipts don't implicate anyone. There's another folder in here with pictures of the same kids at 'time of purchase,' which should help prove this isn't just a collection of missing person stats. But even if this somehow leads to arrests, Stark has likely done quite a lot to distance himself from this ring. There's nothing assuring that he will go down with the ship."

"Are you saying this could all be for nothing? This horrible thing that's been happening under our noses for decades keeps happening, my father keeps living his perfect life, and I have to figure out how to live my life knowing the man who made me is a fucked-up, repulsive piece of shit?"

"That's not what he's saying," I assured her, not actually sure of that fact.

"I'm saying that's a possibility." Donovan was clearly less interested in comforting Jolie than I was. "Another possibility is that it gets taken down, but your father remains unscathed. Another possibility is that we make sure he doesn't."

Finally, I was catching up to my partner. "All right. Then we make sure this evidence is tied to Stark. How do we do that?"

He cleared his throat, and I could tell that the pause wasn't to give him time to think of the answer but meant to slow his brain down so he could bring us up to speed. "Financial records would be helpful. His large bank deposits don't line up with these receipts, either in amount or timing, but over a decade, the totals come close enough to be suspicious, particularly when we're adding in expenses he might have paid in cash such as purchase of a boat or a vacation home. He's been careful on purpose. He's been smart.

"If he was found with copies of these folders—the bills of sale along with the photos sent back from those who made the purchase—that would be quite incriminating. As I said, he might already have this. Do you know where he'd keep information like this?"

"His safe at the cabin." She looked toward me. "Did you see anything when you got into it?"

Christ, that was seventeen years ago.

She had the same thought. "It might have been actual papers. Or a floppy disc."

"I don't remember what else was in there," I said honestly. "All I was interested in was the cash."

It would have to be planted there then. To be sure.

"So you know the combo?" Donovan asked, picking up on the fact I'd opened the cabin safe before.

"It's not the same safe," Jolie said before I could reply. "He replaced it after the money was gone. The new safe has the same combo—because that's how original he is—but now it requires a key to get in as well. At least, that was what he had a decade ago. It's probably still the same. He's particular and doesn't like things to change."

Donovan seemed to be taking notes in his head. "Let's assume then that the combination is the same. Do you know where the key is kept?"

"There are two keys. He keeps one on his key ring. The other is locked in a drawer in his home office." She rubbed her eyes, the lack of sleep likely catching up with her.

"The cabin's in Sherman, right?" Donovan had done his research. "And the home office in Wallingford. What's that—an hour away?"

"An hour and a half." I remembered the drive well.

"It's going to be a task for a PI to get into the house where your father lives and then get into the cabin safe. Not impossible, but there are easier ways to do this." He was leading us to suggest it ourselves, so that he wouldn't have to.

And I didn't want Jolie to be the one either. "I should do it."

"It will be just as hard for you to break in as a PI," she said.

The cabin wouldn't be hard. It was the house that would be tricky, and we both knew it. "I won't break in."

Her head snapped toward me. "You're planning on just going up and knocking? You don't even know if they'll let you in."

"They'll let me in." Like I'd been doing all morning, I pretended I was more sure of that than I was.

She turned away, her finger running back and forth over her lip while she deliberated with herself. "It should be me."

"I don't want it to be you."

She shifted again to face me. "This whole thing started with me. This is my responsibility."

"Bringing Donovan in was my idea. You had no idea it would lead to this."

"Neither did you."

I opened my mouth to offer another protest, but she beat me to speaking. "They'll let *me* in."

They would. I knew it in my gut. Whatever falling out she'd had with her father, he'd always allow her to return. There'd be a price, but he'd let her pay it.

She knew that as well as I did.

And I knew that she'd made up her mind. That she'd decided this. That there would be no chance of talking her out of it.

"I'll go with you," I said, and it was settled. I was as decided as she was.

She didn't argue. "I need to cancel my flight and get a sub. Let me make a couple of calls." She plucked her cell phone out of her purse and walked out of the office.

By the time the door shut behind her, Donovan was

handing me a flash drive. "I put the relevant files on here. It has an amnesiac installed on it so there will be no log of where the data came from."

I didn't know if I was more impressed that he'd managed the transfer so quickly or that he just happened to have an untraceable USB drive hanging around his office.

I took it from him without comment. He didn't need a bigger head than he already had.

"You're not driving with me to Connecticut," he said, reminding me he was also heading to the state for the weekend.

"Didn't ask." Washington and Wallingford weren't even on the same route. "We'll take the train. We can rent a car when we get there."

He nodded his approval. "You can borrow one of mine if you'd like. I'm taking the Tesla."

"Thanks for the offer, but I think we'd be better off if we were a little less conspicuous." And if our next stop was the cabin, I doubted his luxury vehicles could handle the mountain snow.

"I'm sure you're right." He looked thoughtful. "Is this going to be dangerous?"

We were adults now. Before today, I'd have said that Stark couldn't hold the same physical power over us that he once had.

Now that I knew how deep he was involved with the crime world, I felt less certain. "I'll take your gun."

Of course even with a gun, there was a mental risk to returning home. For both of us.

Donovan stood and picked up the coat he'd thrown over his chair when he arrived and took it to the closet to hang up. While he was there, he retrieved ours.

"I don't need to tell you to be careful," he said, handing

them to me. A not-so-subtle cue that it was time to leave. "But I will tell you, while you're gone, I have something you should think about."

I took the coats and picked up Jolie's purse from the floor. "What's that?"

"Where you're going to put that new tattoo."

I didn't change gears as fast as he did, so it took me a second to understand what he was implicating. "How could you possibly know that—?" I cut myself off too late. I'd already confessed. "You know what? Fuck you." But also, I appreciated his attempt to lighten the mood. The morning had been heavy, to say the least.

"Yeah, yeah, yeah." He slapped me on the back as he ushered me out his door. "It's going to be a terribly embarrassing tattoo, Cade. Even so, you're going to think it was worth it."

As much as I hated it when Donovan was right, I had a feeling he wasn't wrong.

TWENTY-EIGHT

I t wasn't until we were waiting in line at Avis in Grand Central that I had a chance to really think about what we were doing, what we were about to do. We were two hours away from where everything between us had started, and even with the drive ahead of us, I worried we didn't have enough time to form a plan. Or that we'd forgotten something. I wondered if we should stop and think.

But I also knew that given the chance to deliberate, I might not be able to force myself to go through with it. Acting quickly helped give me momentum. Jolie gave me the motivation. As much as I wished she hadn't decided to walk into hell with me, I recognized that I needed her at my side.

"You were able to change your flight?" I asked when I needed to get out of my head.

"Yeah. I had to pay a fee to cancel it. They gave me a credit that I can use later for my trip back home."

"Did you have enough to pay that? I can—"

"Stop." She nudged me with her shoulder as she said it, stepping closer to do so and staying closer afterward. "You've given me way too much this week, which I appreciate, but no. I'm good. I got paid today. Which means I'm paying for the rental car."

I started to protest because that was ridiculous, but she didn't let me. "Please? It will make me feel like I'm contributing."

It took a beat for me to wrestle through the urge to put my foot down, and another beat to consider what it meant that I needed to care for her so badly. And one more to decide it would be in my best interest to refuse that desire. "Just the car rental. Everything else is on me."

Then it was our turn to step up to the rental desk. The agent rattled off a memorized spiel about our options, not trying very hard to upsell us when we decided on the standard SUV rather than the premium. After fully grilling him, I felt confident the tires would make it up to the cabin, even if it snowed, and then it was time for Jolie to hand over her credit card and license.

Without hesitation, she opened her purse and pulled out her wallet. It was only after she'd opened it up that she paused. "Uh, Cade. I saw a vending machine in the hall outside. Would you mind grabbing me a water?"

"Here's one, complimentary." The agent pulled a warm bottle out from under his desk.

Her smile was uneasy. "It's okay. I'd prefer cold, if you don't mind."

"I'll take the warm one," I said, picking it up off the counter. "And I'll get you one that's cold. Watch my bag."

The agent stopped me. "Your license, sir! If you want to be listed as a driver, I'll need to see a valid license."

"He can probably enter in your info while you're getting my water," Jolie said as I pulled out my wallet and dropped my ID on the counter.

"I can," the man confirmed.

I glanced suspiciously at the agent, fighting off an unreasonable flash of jealousy. If the guy hadn't been as old as her father, I might have thought she was trying to get rid of me. "Must really be thirsty."

"Parched."

I left her and found the vending machine quickly, returning to the ticket counter just as the agent was handing over the paperwork. Jolie seemed tense, which was reasonable, considering where we were headed.

"Here's your cards," the agent said, pushing them over the counter. "And your keys. Enjoy your trip, Mr. and Mrs. Warren."

I chuckled as I reached for my ID, chiding myself for how natural the pairing sounded, and expected Jolie to refute it. When she didn't, busying herself with putting her ID and credit card away instead, I chided myself for thinking that might mean something.

But then in her haste, she dropped her license to the ground, and even though she rushed to grab it, I beat her to it.

I glanced at it as I handed it over, because of course I did, and when she snatched it out of my hand, it was too late. I'd already seen it. Her name. The first was Jolie, as she'd insisted it was, not Julianna. And her last name didn't say Stark. It said Warren.

She didn't look at me, slipping her ID in her wallet and her wallet in her purse. Organizing the paperwork the agent had given her and stuffing it in her bag as well, along with the cold water I'd brought her.

"Jolie *Warren*?" I hadn't ever put those two names together.

No, maybe I had. Years ago. When we were plotting our escape, but I hadn't said it enough to get used to the way it felt in my mouth. The way it rolled over my tongue.

The color seeped out of her face. She refused to look at me. "We're holding up the line."

Grabbing the handle of her suitcase, she towed it behind her as she headed out the door that led to the parking lot.

I jammed my license in my pocket and followed after. It was obvious she didn't want to discuss what I'd seen, but there was no way I was letting it go. "Why does your ID say my last name?"

She stopped outside to scan down the rows of cars. "G-3, G-3," she said, searching for where our vehicle was parked.

"Jolie?"

"I told you I changed my name so my father couldn't find me." She still wouldn't look at me. "Do you see row G?"

Fuck row G. "Why did you pick Warren? Out of all the names you could have picked. Why Warren?"

She let out a puff of air, her shoulders sagging in resignation before she turned to face me. "Because it was who I wanted to be, okay? I told you already."

I held her gaze, trying to find something in her eyes that could explain that to me. Could explain how she could refuse to leave with me and then seven years later choose my name as the one she wanted to live by. How she could then disappear. How she wouldn't seek me out until ten more years had passed.

She'd wrecked me when she'd told me she didn't want me. Why was she living like I'd been the one who wrecked her?

"You won't understand," she said, breaking our stare.

"I want to."

"I know you do. I just." She rubbed her hands over her face. Took a deep breath. Put herself back together. "Can we deal with this first? With my dad?"

It wasn't fair. It was never fair, how she got to set the terms. How I was always paying interest. How the balance never changed.

I couldn't keep doing it.

I wouldn't.

But fuck. Her bringing down her father required all our focus. And it wasn't just about us anymore.

"After your dad is dealt with, we talk." It wasn't a request.

It would give me time, too. To figure out what should happen next with us. Maybe by then I'd be able to admit what I wanted. "I mean it, Jolie. I need answers."

"We'll talk," she agreed, her tone heavy, as though the commitment would be hard to keep.

Her weariness made it easier to believe that she meant to follow through, at least. It didn't make waiting any less frustrating.

Snatching the keys out of her hand, I nodded to the right. "Row G. I'm driving."

When we found the SUV, I got her into the passenger seat before putting our bags in the back. We only had one each, so it didn't take long, but I took the opportunity to open up my suitcase and get Donovan's gun out of the hard-cased container he'd given me for transport. After loading the cartridge, I shoved it in my coat pocket.

"Everything okay back there?"

"Yep. Just digging out my sunglasses." I grabbed those from the side pocket of my bag and shut the hatch.

A few minutes later we were on the road. Once out of the city, it was a straightforward route, which made the drive easy, and though I wanted to push her about her name and her secrets, I forced myself to spend the time firming up our plan. We decided to say we'd both been in New York—me for a wedding, her for a weekend away—sticking to the truth for the most part. *"Seeing each other again took us down memory lane, and we decided on a whim to drive up to the academy."* We expected they'd entertain us in the living room. The conversation would be awkward and painful, especially painful for us. At some point, I'd excuse myself to use the restroom and slip into his office to get the key.

Jolie said she should be the one to do the snooping because she knew what the key looked like and where it was kept.

I argued that I was the one who knew how to pick a lock. Plus, it had been ten years, and everything might be different. He might have moved it.

Besides, if I was caught, I was the one who could defend myself. I didn't mention I had a gun on me.

She agreed reluctantly, then suggested we should both have our phones on so we could text each other if need be.

And if nothing went as planned, we'd improvise.

I preferred being more prepared; I didn't know if it even mattered. Honestly, I was still not entirely convinced we'd even be let in.

Once we crossed the city limits of Wallingford, we grew quiet. There was too much to take in outside of us. The roads that had changed. The parts of town that had expanded. The stores that were gone. The new stores in their place. It was an odd thing to return to haunted ground. The shape of the city had altered enough to almost convince myself the ghosts were gone. That they had never existed in the first place.

But then we were turning on the winding drive that led to Stark Academy, and each bend of the road was so achingly familiar, I could navigate the SUV with my eyes shut.

And closing my eyes was tempting. Because each sight held a memory, and each memory led down a spiral of emotions. Emotions too tangled to unravel.

I couldn't imagine how much worse it had to be for Jolie. Stark had only been my home for a year. It had been hers for most of her life.

Whatever she was feeling, she managed to put a mask on. Her face was unreadable as we passed the turnoff toward the main entrance in favor of the less-driven road that curled behind the boarding school, past the cook's residence and the gardener's and the lodgings for visitors and prospective students, ending at the three-story house at the back of the property.

I parked the car, careful not to block the garage—a habit that was beaten into me—but when I pulled the key from the ignition, neither of us moved to get out.

"I should go in first." She looked suddenly nervous. More nervous, since she'd been low-key fidgety the entire trip. "You know, in case...in case..."

"In case...what?"

She took a deep breath, then shrugged. "I just wonder what they'll bring up."

I almost laughed. Whatever they used to hold against us, it couldn't compare to their sins. Even with what I didn't know about Jolie and the years before she'd left Wallingford, I couldn't imagine she had anything to be ashamed of.

Stark would try, though. And it would be hard to listen to, so I didn't say anything.

"What do you think she'll say to you?"

I'd tried not to think about *her*. Now that I allowed the thought, I didn't know what to expect. "She might not say anything at all."

"It was always too big of a house for just me and my dad. When he got married again, it almost felt snug enough to be a home."

I nodded.

"What if they aren't home?"

"Then we'll wait."

"What if they don't let us in?"

"Then we'll come back when it's dark." I wondered for the billionth time if we should skip the face-to-face and just sneak in later, but then there was an alarm to navigate, and Jolie's father had always been a light sleeper.

She turned to look at me. "Is it surreal to be back here? Like out of a dream?"

"Like out of a nightmare, more like."

"Yeah. That's it. Except, with you here, it's not him I'm scared of. I'm scared of not getting what we need."

It was hard to admit, even to myself, that I was scared too. But I was more scared of the woman sitting next to me, of losing her all over again. That was always the nightmare. A recurring one over the years that I realized in that moment could very well come true.

Not giving myself time to overthink it, I took her hand and

squeezed. "We'll get it. If we don't, we'll try again until he goes down."

"Okay."

"Okay."

I let go of her hand, stowed my sunglasses, and at the same time, we both pushed open our doors. Side by side, we walked up the stone steps to the front door.

Jolie hesitated, her hand stretched out above the handle. "Do we ring the bell or just walk in?"

It seemed odd as fuck to ring. "Maybe knock?"

Turned out she didn't have to. The door opened on its own, and there stood a woman I hadn't seen in seventeen years.

She looked Jolie over for half a second. Looked longer at me. "About time you came in. I thought you might sit in the car all evening. Just the two of you?" She wiped her hands on her apron, a newer one than she'd had when I was a kid, but a similar style, and peered behind us as if expecting there were more ghosts from her past waiting to haunt her.

Instinctively, I peered too, my eyes following her gaze to the empty car. She got her answer faster from looking before I could summon up one with words. "Dinner's almost ready. There should be enough."

Jolie glanced at me, her expression showing even less confidence than she'd shown in the car.

I offered a tight smile and hoped it was encouraging. Truth was, my stomach had turned into a knotted rope, and every breath I tried to take in went shallow.

"Hi, Carla," Jolie said, and I had to give her credit for not calling her mom. Her father had required that she did when he'd remarried, an expectation that she'd fulfilled even though she'd hated it.

But instead of completely snubbing her with the dropped title, Jolie leaned in and gave her a half hug that was surprisingly returned before she walked inside past her.

I couldn't bring myself to be that affectionate. It already felt like I was on the verge of losing my grip, a grip I'd never been sure I had in the first place.

But I did address her as I walked past, using the name I'd called her once upon a time. Before Wallingford. Before Langdon Stark. "Hi, Mom."

Then I followed Jolie into the house where it all began, where I'd spent the best and worst year of my life being beaten by my stepdad and falling in love with his daughter.

Cade and Jolie's love story continues in
Wild War
book two in the epic Dirty Wild trilogy

PAIGE PRESS

Paige Press isn't just Laurelin Paige anymore...

Laurelin Paige has expanded her publishing company to bring readers even more hot romances.

Sign up for our newsletter to get the latest news about our releases and receive a free book from one of our amazing authors:

Stella Gray
CD Reiss
Jenna Scott
Raven Jayne
JD Hawkins
Poppy Dunne

ALSO BY LAURELIN PAIGE

Visit my website for a more detailed reading order.

The Dirty Universe
Dirty Filthy Rich Boys - READ FREE

Dirty Duet (Donovan Kincaid)
Dirty Filthy Rich Men | Dirty Filthy Rich Love

Dirty Games Duet (Weston King)
Dirty Sexy Player| Dirty Sexy Games

Dirty Sweet Duet (Dylan Locke)
Sweet Liar | Sweet Fate

(Nate Sinclair) Dirty Filthy Fix (a spinoff novella)

Dirty Wild Trilogy (Cade Warren)
Wild Rebel | Wild War | Wild Heart

Man in Charge Duet
Man in Charge

Man in Love

Man for Me (a spinoff novella)

The Fixed Universe

Fixed Series (Hudson & Alayna)

Fixed on You | Found in You | Forever with You | Hudson | Fixed Forever

Found Duet (Gwen & JC) Free Me | Find Me

(Chandler & Genevieve) Chandler (a spinoff novella)

(Norma & Boyd) Falling Under You (a spinoff novella)

(Nate & Trish) Dirty Filthy Fix (a spinoff novella)

Slay Series (Celia & Edward)

Rivalry | Ruin | Revenge | Rising

(Gwen & JC) The Open Door (a spinoff novella)

(Camilla & Hendrix) Slash (a spinoff novella)

First and Last

First Touch | Last Kiss

Hollywood Standalones

One More Time

Close

Sex Symbol

Star Struck

ABOUT LAURELIN PAIGE

With millions of books sold, Laurelin Paige is the NY Times, Wall Street Journal, and USA Today Bestselling Author of the Fixed Trilogy. She's a sucker for a good romance and gets giddy anytime there's kissing, much to the embarrassment of her three daughters. Her husband doesn't seem to complain, however. When she isn't reading or writing sexy stories, she's probably singing, watching shows like Killing Eve, Letterkenny, and Discovery of Witches, or dreaming of Michael Fassbender. She's also a proud member of Mensa International though she doesn't do anything with the organization except use it as material for her bio.

www.laurelinpaige.com
laurelinpaigeauthor@gmail.com

CPSIA information can be obtained
at www.ICGtesting.com
Printed in the USA
LVHW032130080421
683868LV00002B/226

9 781953 520241